I0621905

DIAMONDS

BLONDES

AND

POISON

A Wright Series

Book 1

Linda McKown

Diamonds Blondes and Poison
ISBN-13: 978-0-9997357-0-1

Author:
LindaMcKownAuthor LLC
11574 E Running Deer Trail
Scottsdale, AZ 85262
http://www.lindamckown.com

Any names of people and entities are fictitious in this story
having been created by the author's imagination.

Front Cover Photo of the book is copyright through
Shutterstock. Book title manipulation was done by Joseph
McKown

DIAMONDS BLONDES AND POISON

Dedicated to my husband Joe and my sons, Ryan and Greg

Contents

1   Napa

JESS JAMESON DROVE her rental car across the San Francisco Bay Golden Gate Bridge toward Napa, California. It was a familiar drive. Looking down at the water below, she saw sailboats racing with the wind billowing their sails. She speculated her friend, Dean Crain, was probably on the water today. Her friend loved the energy of the wind. Once Dean motored his boat away from the Oakland docks, he unfurled his sails, and the wind didn't dare to not appear. Wishing she was on his pretty sleek boat, she left a message on his cell phone to remind him she was going to Napa for vacation. She took one last look at the beams of the bridge and liked the contrast. The International Orange paint was specifically chosen to create the color play. The orange blended well with the countryside. The bridge became an icon for its inhabitants and an enjoyable view while crossing to Marin County.

She was approaching the Marin County hills as she exited the bridge. It was an affluent area and popular with the tourists who came to visit Muir Woods, Stinson Beach, or the Point Reyes Lighthouse. She smiled, because the Point Reyes National Seashore was one of her favorite areas for taking photographs. The redwoods in Muir Woods were her second favorite attraction. She would save some of her vacation to visit one of the places, because Napa was her current focus. Napa was the main attraction on this trip.

Jess laughed remembering her friend. Dean Crain, an elderly gentleman and good friend, who showed her the sites of San Francisco. He took her to the wharf, where they ate fresh seafood out of paper cups and watched seals on the rafts. Perusing the museums, they saw old, very large, beautiful oil paintings. He took her to the tourist shops and bought her jade jewelry. The diamond exchange was checked out. Using his poker winnings, a stunning gray single pearl necklace with diamonds was a surprise for her birthday. A ghost restaurant was exciting one evening when they drove south from San Francisco along the coast. They sat outside with covered blankets, sipping their after-dinner coffee. The evening sky dimmed, and the stars came out. Both were disappointed when no ghost appeared. Jess told him, "The ghost wasn't there anymore." She knew it disappeared.

Dean couldn't help himself. The day with Jess had been good. He looked over at her snuggled in a wool blanket. The fringe surrounding her blonde hair made her look like a model in a cover magazine. He said, "No way."

"Yes, believable. You must know?"

"Okay, I give, what must I know?" He waved his hands in the air like a wand, wishing the bewitched ghosts to appear. He glanced at the other restaurant patrons. They were wishing the same thing.

Jess scrunched up her face at him. "There's an easy explanation. Ghosts couldn't live forever on our earth. They ran into problems with our atmosphere. The laws of gravity broke down around a ghost body. The more remote the ghost body was from earth, the more it lost its hold. Then the ghost drifted away into the night much like the way a con artist vanishes."

Dean told her, "You're beyond the normal." It was a compliment. She made him laugh.

They wandered through gigantic redwood trees located north in Muir Woods. Jess brought her camera gear and was glued to her lenses the whole time. Dean didn't think she saw the trees until she gave him three framed photos for his birthday. There were so much more than the trees. Light- and dark- colored leaves catching dew in between towering branches were the images. She captured the soul of the old trees. Dean was pleased. He saw the complicated woman in those photos. It was her signature.

Waiting patiently while she tried on soft pima cotton sundresses and matching sandals, he purchased them for her to leave on his sailboat. Then she could stay any time. She ordered him captain's hats from around the world. He wore the hats when they cruised out of the bay. His crew knew all about Jess. Dean was happy whenever she was onboard. There was laughter, excitement, and fun. The chef knew to prepare vegetarian as part of the meal course. Dean's crew treated all his guests with courtesy and professionalism, especially her.

Dean showed her the better eclectic dance bars his daughter frequented when she was alive. One of the bars was Caribbean calypso music. She went crazy dancing with one of the patrons putting on a fantastic show. She matched the intricate dance steps with her partner so that people cleared the floor to watch. Dean dragged her the next day to a music store and let her find her perfect song. It was number six on his seventy-five-foot sailboat sound system. There was a number seven song, but most of the time on the sailboat cruise, she hit number six. His crew loved the sound, because Jess would let go and dance on the boat deck looking like a magical, ethereal free spirit. The crew started walking the calypso dance in their work routine.

Dean missed his daughter very much, having lost her to an overdose of drugs. He called Jess "darling" once. No one ever called her that name. She asked Dean about the word. He told her that's what he called his daughter. It meant beloved. He felt the same way about her.

Jess lived through a little difficulty. She learned at an early age to trust no one. Her father disappeared from life after her mother's death. Jess didn't know how to help him. Being an only child made her lean more toward a self-sufficient nature. She became more independent and carried the weight of responsibility of the adult world upon her shoulders. That lack of trust would move her away from people. Jess would try to handle everything, except there were things she couldn't do, and she must trust someone. Dean became the person she trusted.

Upon her arrival in Napa, she saw several wine stores. She thought it would be a good idea to check the local wineries she knew if there was time. Driving down the main thoroughfare of Napa, she turned the corner. Seeing the jewelry in the window and then the large sign, she knew she arrived at her destination. The rental car was parked across the street.

First, she ordered a tuna salad sandwich and soda at the quaint restaurant as she sat at one of the outside tables. There was a slight warm summer breeze today as she watched tourists bustling in and out of the trinket and T-shirt shops. It made a parade of color in all sizes and shapes. Children were bouncing along the pavement from too much rainbow snow cones. She heard the vintage train whistle in the distance. It was the wine train tour that went to Helena and back.

Tossing her wrapper and empty containers in the garbage, she went across the street to the jewelry store to check the place out and see if the building blueprints matched. While in the store, she looked around until a man in his mid-twenties came up to her. He saw a pretty blonde woman and thought she looked like a good prospect to sell the store's jewelry to. He noticed she was looking at diamond necklaces.

"Good afternoon, my name is Bill Barker. Can I help you find a diamond necklace?"

"Yes, I'm interested in the Fancy Violet Gray necklace."

"You must know diamonds because most people would not have known the color name. It's a perfect match to your beautiful eyes." He pulled out the mist-colored necklace.

Jess looked at the small stoned necklace and told him. "It is lovely. Can I see the other two necklaces?"

Pretending to examine the necklaces within the sixteen-thousand-dollar range, she moved as close as she could to the two-hundred-fifty-thousand-dollar diamond necklace without attracting the salesperson's attention to the priceless object. She quickly glanced at its case which was under a series of overhead light canisters. The light was aimed at the gray velvet mannequin head to enhance the glitter fire sparkle of the precious cut stones.

The diamonds were matched exactly in size, color, and brilliance on each side from the center of the necklace. The original designer was an artist finding such perfectly matched stones. They looked better than she remembered in their platinum setting. The necklace's interesting clasp design made it unique. The necklace was an exact match to the one she held briefly in her hands when an elderly lady brought it into a small shop in Los Angeles. It was the very same necklace.

Jess thanked the sales clerk, "I'll be back."

"I would be glad to welcome someone who obviously loves diamonds. You could always special order anything you desire. It is a pity we do not have any colored stones like the Darya-ye Noor."

"The pink diamond, one of the largest in the world, is very beautiful in the pictures. It would be impossible to find a stone today with such colorful brilliance. But you never know what the earth can cough up or what has been secreted away for centuries," said Jess.

"You are knowledgeable about diamonds, too. It is an interesting story. The stone has changed hands many times and not always willingly."

"Yes, I know the story. Where large diamonds are involved, there is always a tale about any exchange. Some stories contain facts and some history gets lost, accidentally, of course."

The clerk was suddenly very interested in this new tourist. She was bright, indeed. "Accidentally is probably an understatement. Do you need directions to your hotel?"

"No, it's just a couple miles down the road."

Returning the next day, she asked, "Can I see the Fancy Violet Gray diamond necklace once more?"

The same young sales clerk waited on her again.

"Which hotel did you say you're staying? Was it the White Heron Hotel or The Old Gaslight Inn?"

Jess looked askance at the nosy young man. "I hadn't really said which one."

He saw her concern and hastily replied, "Oh, no problem. Both were good hotels. You should enjoy yourself in their excellent wine shops. I'm very familiar with the local wineries if you need any help there. Or if you want good food, I know exactly where the best restaurants are in town and can show you. All you need to do is say the word, and I'll be available. I hope you will return to see the necklaces again. It's nice to talk to you."

Jess left the building and paused on the corner. "I didn't mean to attract the man's attention." She had talked too much. Worrying about the sales clerk, she moved toward the restaurant.

Sitting across the street, she sat with her latte coffee watching everyone and everything. Taking a bite of her raisin scone, she annotated in her special shorthand code all the information on her small personal computer notebook. The keyboard was red which she liked very much. She wondered why they didn't make the keyboard a swirly red with a touch of pink. The sales for that item would have been astronomical. Most women would compare the colorful keyboard to another favorite accessory, like super expensive and tall, absolutely must-have, six-inch heels. Jess laughed. She was riding the wave crest of her high thoughts. Her imagination always took her off to a different wavelength. Did other woman think the way she did? No, Jess knew that she was one of a kind.

If anyone stopped to ask what she was doing, she explained she was writing a book about the history of grapes. Talking about the mission fathers who brought the grapes to Sonoma around the 1800's, she explained that the locals long ago called them mission grapes. Later there were the gold rush farmers who planted grapes because farming was more profitable than panning. The tourist would yawn and quickly leave because they came to Napa to drink the grape. History was a passé subject unless a person was on vacation on a bus tour in New York City. The appeal of her explanation to the Napa tourist was about as interesting as watching a gorilla crush a tin cup at the zoo. Jess crushed her empty paper cup and threw it in the trash.

"I made it, good shot today. I've missed the shot the last two times. It must be my lucky day."

It was time to get serious. She noted all the in-store information and then the external such as security cameras, store owners, tourists, buses, cars, even how long the stoplights worked. This was her last jewelry heist, and then she could retire to this small group of islands. She already purchased a tiny and very old cottage there with a friend's help under a different company name. Jess drove to the small hotel in Napa.

Everyday Jess ate breakfast, lunch, and dinner at the small restaurant across the street from the jewelry store. She did this routine for two more days repeating the same watchful lookout process. Then it would be time to hide the blueprints and dig up her tools and gear. Jess Jameson was there in Napa to steal a diamond necklace, a very specific diamond necklace. It was her family's heirloom stolen from her mother years ago.

She entered the con artist game willingly. The game could be cloaked in deception and high danger. She knew the risks. It didn't matter, Jess was determined to succeed. The diamond necklace was rightfully hers. Nothing and no one was going to stop this secret mission.

Her face and posture sitting at the small outside table reflected a young woman in deep writer's concentration. Jess blended in with the crowd. People wouldn't remember her face. It was her intention. She was ready for the robbery tonight. Her mask and costume would be worn. She would become someone else when she opened the door. Diamond obsession overtook her. Her misty eyes watered for a moment and she shook her head. Emotions weren't allowed. Steel strength was required. She hardened her heart and told herself that everything would be fine. She would be in and out fast.

Jess looked thoroughly at the outside of the jewelry store and its heavy window glass the previous day. Right before the clerks left, she saw one of the store assistants turn off the store's upper inside security cameras. She wondered about that action. Perhaps the manager wasn't worried because the jewels were placed in a large safe and the glass cases were empty. It seemed a cheap mistake. The maintenance cost on those cameras was expensive. The store manager more than likely dropped his maintenance plan on them. It was an unwise decision.

The front and back door had alarms connected to a small, local security company. She knew how to disable those alarms. She had driven by the security company and the door was locked and no one was around. She figured that business was also a little lax in protection. It would seem like a hiccup in the security system door alarms due to the shortness of time off the grid. Jess knew how long it would take her to get into the safe. She also knew where jewelry stores kept the expensive stuff, top shelf always. Jess was confident in her abilities. Opening the safe was a no brainer. It was child's play for her.

Once she stepped through the door of the con artist game, the door would be difficult to close. Everything would come through the door into her world. Jess unknowingly placed herself in harm's way.

2   Con Artist and Game

BEING CONNED AT some point in time is a common occurrence. One person's foreknowledge will give them the edge. This person is the con artist. They jump, silently grabbing the advantage.

Unfortunately for the con artist, they don't know that a person (the conned) have already been there in this perfect spot. There are two people entering a now familiar situation at the same point in time. Another person could be set up to take the fall, the con artist might get away with the heist, or the con artist will fail. Sometimes the conned will be the winner of the game, but that meant the other con artist did fail miserably.

The people in the game pretend by wearing masks and costumes; they become someone else. More people could be hidden from everyone's view with a change of name. The lines of good and bad blur. Which door was opened? Next, more confusion and inexperience enter the ring. Disaster ensues once they become aware of each other.

Dean Crain knew all about con artists. He had been one of the major players in the game. He knew all the industries, department groups, and levels out there. Usually he was involved in the industry of *Stolen Goods*. Why stolen goods? Selling was easy and there was always money involved. A person didn't have to work full time. There was no need to report profits to the government. It was a win-win proposition if a person dared himself to get involved in the venture, plus the glory if you succeeded. The pay purchased fun somewhere else, better toys, or weapons.

In this story, Dean gets pulled back into the game via his relationship with Jess. Her contact with an elderly woman in a jewelry store becomes the catalyst which moves Jess's life in a different direction. The elderly woman, lured into a jewelry store when the adopted son saw their sign of seventy percent off becomes a victim. The ruse by the store owner was to obtain high-end jewelry for them to switch. The owner would keep the jewelry for resale and substitute one which was fake. The illegal exchange was not a business transaction, but it was a con game.

The con game or illegal exchange of jewelry hit the streets of the underground network. The police hear rumors about the scam. Things break open when someone dies. When the fraudulent owners understand that their game is a bust, they close shop, and disappear. They are gone like a nor'easter and the windy cyclone traveling the New England states. The money moves with the criminals as a resource safely guarded. The victims become part of the leftover devastation.

As a person can see, the levels developed in this story are from unsavory, inexperienced newbie to extremely experienced evil. The more the riches or prize, the greater the evil in one of the con artists. If that con artist was not currently evil, the scales tip toward the gates of hell. Obsession happens. The slide toward more evil becomes an unstoppable force for a while. People become caught in the web.

Dean knows that he must help Jess, but finds himself face-to-face with the police and Derek Wright. Warning signs flash into Dean's brain, "Hazardous. Enter at your own risk." Dean knows that eventually, the industry, department groups, and levels will collide which could make things difficult, noisy, and messy. He worries that if all the players open the door, there will be no turning back. So many choices and crossroads pave the paths. The choice currently for Dean and Derek is to *pick a path*.

Jess unknowingly enters the ring. What she hadn't counted on was the obsessive person or persons who would stalk her. That would throw her, and she would need help to find her way. She was the odd-ball person in the game. It wasn't about money for her. She was about passion. She would move with or without people to recover what was her property. The fanfare or police didn't matter to her. It was something the thieves hadn't counted on. Jess had nothing to lose. Her obsession was more powerful, and she couldn't quit the game until she reached her goal.

3   Heist Day

AT MIDNIGHT, HER TV stopped working, and she notified the hotel clerk who came to her room. He fixed the loose cable in the wall outlet. The hotel clerk told Jess he only worked until one in the morning when the relief person would take over. He told her it was a good thing that he was there to fix the TV because Betsy, the relief person, was clueless about such things. Betsy only liked knitting. She did make nice blankets with a grape design and sold them at the better shops and recommended she check out the Yarn Needle shop. Jess was distracted by his conversation about yarn.

"I saw the pretty afghan in the store window when I found the public restrooms. The design was very nice and definitely did highlight the grape-wine theme."

The hotel clerk told her the room TV was working great again. He went back to the office. Waiting a little longer, she went out into the dark of night. After jogging at a fast pace, about two miles from her hotel room to the jewelry store, she stopped. Something was very wrong when she approached the jewelry store that she intended to rob.

The front door was not completely closed. It was not right. This scene was wrong. She felt darkness deeper than the night. The darkness was not a ghost but devious eyes. Evil watched her. She felt strange and in danger. Jess looked around but couldn't see anyone. She backed away and quickly exited the scene.

She hid again her special tools and gear, placing the blueprints in the plastic tube. Covering her items under a large batch of leaves by an oak tree, she swiftly ran back to her hotel room. The dark clothing was removed after she slipped into the room. The television quietly broadcast a local movie. She turned the machine off.

Fixing herself a drink, she thought, *what mess did I step into now? This is not good.*

The feelings she felt at the scene were resonating in her brain.

There was an evil one out there who slipped his thoughts. The person wasn't cautious. If she ran into the person, would she know him? What about all her plans and steps? The time devoted to this one venture represented an extensive amount of work. The lost time took its toll on her social relationships.

Knowing she was safe and everything was now secure, Jess was perplexed, what exactly happened in the jewelry store tonight?

She wanted her necklace. Where could she go from here?

She would have to wait until morning. She knew the cops would be all over the jewelry store and the little restaurant may or may not be open.

Jess awoke the next morning at five o'clock. There was something nagging her brain; it was the store clerk. There was something odd. "Was it his appearance or his mannerisms that bothered her?" She took her notebook out and pulled up the "Grapes History" file and read her notes. "It was both. His eyes were watery like there was an allergy problem and later, his eyes were fine. Strange." After reviewing them, she shut the notebook, took a shower, and got dressed in casual tourist clothes and tennis shoes.

She wore her hair up today in a ponytail with the white tourist hat, looking like she did the first day in Napa. The restaurant opened at seven, so it was safe to start walking. First, she needed to store her photography equipment, believing the rental car was safer than a hotel room. Jess walked and jogged every day as part of her daily routine. She lifted weights at the gym in Los Angeles where she lived, so she looked thin and extremely fit.

Leaving her notebook safely stashed in the trunk of her car along with camera, high-powered lenses, and tripod, she breathed in the fresh morning air. She took pictures the other day of the beach just in case anyone would wonder why she owned such powerful camera lenses. Her night vision, high-powered binoculars were to search out the birds and owls in the area in case anyone asked about those objects.

She started walking down the green tree-lined road. Her black knit jacket was partially zipped because the morning air was still cool. She breathed in the crisp air, filling her lungs. She read somewhere that trees can hold water. "It must be why the air smells so good here in Napa because there are lots of trees. Anyway, it's a gloriously pretty day."

Her side hurt from jogging so fast the previous night. She stopped and placed the earphones on and she listened to her music on the cell phone. She started singing a familiar song, letting the rapturous notes of the song sync with her walking. She walked swinging her head and body. Her arms were moving slowly back and forth. She was pleased that she was still getting in her exercise. Her sunglasses helped stop the bright morning sun. The traffic was still light. Jess kept to the far right of the road walking in the bike path. As she moved closer, she saw the flashing cop lights on the jeep-style vehicle and several other vehicles. There was a fire truck and ambulance. People were mingling together in small groups of shop owners. She pocketed her phone and sunglasses. A frown creased her brow.

"Is someone hurt? Why is the ambulance there?" she said.

A policeman used yellow tape to cordon off the whole area. The owner of the restaurant was conversing with the police. Another cop approached her and said, "Sorry, Miss, the restaurant would be closed all day today."

Jess was going to ask what happened, but the ambulance crew came out with a body covered totally up.

Jess said, "Oh, dear, someone died."

"Miss, you need to leave. The area is closed."

Jess turned and started to jog back to her hotel. Wanting to put distance between herself and the dead body, she finally turned the jog into a walk. Because her side still hurt, she held onto her left side. A dark sedan was approaching on the road and pulled over. A tall good-looking man dressed in dark suit, white shirt, and gray tie stepped out of the vehicle. He ran his hands through his brown hair. His brown eyes suddenly lit up.

Jess Jameson, was that really the girl he knew? An amazing coincidence. What in the world was she doing in Napa?

Meanwhile, Jess was thinking, *Oh, no, not the nice Los Angeles investigator guy.* The person was the very familiar Mr. Wright who worked with the police. He entered her world and knocked it off the center of gravity. She tried to move her world as far away from Derek as possible. There was no time in her life for desire or passion. She could not get serious about anyone until this business was completed.

Jess slowly approached the car on the other side of the road.

"Hello, Derek, how are things? What brings you to Napa?"

As if she didn't already know the answer to her own question. He was here because of the dead body.

His six-foot muscled body leaned against the dark sedan as if he had all day. He knew about the very dead body and thought things could wait a few minutes. Jess was this gorgeous young girl who came into his life one day when he stopped to help her change a flat tire. He looked her over. She was blonde, beautiful all the way, and every man's dream come true. She had curves in all the right places. She massively rocked his world. He remembered every minute of their encounter.

He wanted to touch her now, but knew to wait. Jess was worth the wait. The low light from the ascending sun hit a strand of her hair that escaped her cap. Jess's hair became golden. Derek acknowledged the fire he felt for her increased exponentially beyond total repair. He was lost in her every movement. Her eyes were almost soft blue-gray this morning. He liked her eyes--no, he liked all of her. All he desired was her. Derek felt out of control.

After two dates, he thought things were going great. Derek knew he was a bright, handsome, good-looking, eligible male specimen. He knew his share of beautiful women in the past. Jess met other equally interesting male friends. Her knowledge of how to kiss was excellent. He remembered the touch of her body against his skin. The two of them were experienced in the dating world.

She gave him that amazing first lingering kiss. It was the kiss that promised him the world. Derek wished he was part of that world. She was sweet and full of passion. Then she dumped him cold, flatter than any girl ever had. He hadn't quite figured out why she walked away from his love. He didn't know how to react to that cold fact.

Derek crossed his arms and responded tentatively, "I asked you first."

"I'm on vacation in the wonderful wine country, taking photo shots. I want to capture Point Reyes soon, because those spectacular photos seemed to be hot sellers. The gallery wants more photos. Having been in the area before shooting the vineyards and grapes, I'm collecting some history on Napa for a book."

Derek remembered her apartment and some of her photos. They were nice and peaceful, mostly late evening or early morning shots with fog or mist. Her eyes at times looked like gray misty pools whenever he held her closely. He noticed her hand.

16

"Are you okay? I saw you holding your side."

"I felt a bad muscle spasm a way back, but it seemed to be better. My desire to stay fit by jogging every day brings them on if I forget to do my stretching exercise first. It was nice talking to you, but I'm detaining you from your work." Jess moved to leave.

Derek moved away from the sedan and came closer. "Where are you staying?"

"The Old Gaslight Inn. The complex has yellow buildings and green doors. It was an older, quiet, and comfortable hotel. They only serve continental breakfast, so I try to find some in town. There seems to be a problem there with police near the restaurant. I'll try a restaurant in the other direction."

"I just passed your hotel a couple miles ago. I would love to go to breakfast with you to talk about your book, but I must keep an appointment in Napa. Can I buy you dinner this evening? We could catch up on our busy lives."

Jess absolutely knew she should say no, but she wanted information. "Great, I would like that. Pick me up at seven. I'm in Room Nineteen."

Derek smiled because she said those words. "It's a date. I'll pick you up at seven."

He handed her one of his business cards in case she lost the old one and Jess did the same.

"I work at a different jewelry store now in Los Angeles. But you forgot to answer my question. Why are you here in Napa?"

"The police believed this case was connected to one I'm currently working in Los Angeles. I'm driving to the Napa Jewelry store."

Jess moved her thin, agile frame to the side of the road allowing him to continue to the murder scene.

He reluctantly left her. Derek couldn't believe his good luck and hadn't expected to meet her so soon. He knew he accidentally fell into the strange meeting with Jess. Maybe fate, chance, or the gods were in his favor. He went to the murder scene in a good mood.

She opened the beautiful door to him. He planned to restore any atmosphere around Jess that would make her fall in love with him. Too bad it was surrounding a burglary and murder investigation. He didn't care what circumstance happened; he won a date with his dream girl. She was important. Jess was what he needed. Derek stepped inside his sedan, smiling, and drove to the murder scene.

4   Jewelry Store Manager's House

DEREK WALKED UP to the local cop in charge and said, "Derek Wright, the Los Angeles investigator hired to research any findings at the scene for the police."

"Who was the victim?"

Derek flashed his credentials.

"I'm here because they believed this murder is connected to another one in my town."

The local cop introduced himself, "Harry Simms."

"The victim was George Beacon, the jewelry store manager, shot execution style in the head and then two in the torso, and one in the groin with a thirty-eight pistol. Coroner thought the head shot was the cause, but we will have to wait for the autopsy. The police search warrant was obtained so they could review the security tapes."

Derek looked at the dead body and thought, *Poor guy.* "What did he do to deserve a death sentence?"

"Anything stolen?"

"We have Bill Barker who worked part-time in the store as a jewelry clerk. If you want to take him in there to check things out, that would be all right. The normal supervisor was out of town, so Bill was it for questions until the supervisor appeared."

"Had anyone notified next of kin?"

Simms responded, "We were trying to locate his wife, but she seemed to be missing."

"Missing? Then let's get a trace on her vehicle if it's not at their house."

"Rutherford was already on it. She likes to dig into a case."

Bill Barker went with Derek into the jewelry store. Bill explained the silent alarm was triggered about midnight. The security company didn't respond until one thirty in the morning.

"I'll check back with you for clarification as to why the security company was so late in responding?"

Bill said, "I know the answer. One of their employees was outside in his car with his girlfriend instead of inside the company. I know the person and called him this morning for information. My supervisor asked me to do that."

"Not good. No, not at all."

Derek and Bill looked in the open vault. Both men seemed surprised. Most of the store jewelry was still there.

Bill wrote down the missing items and handed the paper to Derek.

Derek read, "A forty-six-carat white diamond necklace for two hundred fifty thousand dollars, an eighteen-carat diamond bracelet for sixty thousand dollars, a man's diamond watch for seventy-five thousand dollars, and five-carat diamond ring worth two hundred forty-five thousand dollars. That just didn't make any sense. Someone killed the jewelry store manager for six hundred thirty thousand dollars?"

"Yep, sure looked that way," responded Bill.

Derek looked out the front door and said, "Unless someone or something scared them off. Perhaps they decided to leave to avoid detection. Missing wife, dead husband, and stolen jewelry. Wonder if there was a mistress or a lover? How many were involved?"

It was time to check a few facts with Simms, see the coroner, and visit the jewelry store manager's house.

Derek reached George Beacon's house on Vineyard Lane. He talked with the coroner and the shot to the head was the killing bullet. He turned that piece of information over to his superiors. The house was a two story in the country with large circular paver driveway, four-car garage, and fenced backyard pool. No one was on the property, except the police.

"Nice pad. Napa real estate was expensive. Did a jewelry store manager make enough money to afford this home?"

He waited only a few more minutes and Detective Sally Rutherford came with Simms to the yellow taped house. Rutherford talked to Derek. "There was no sign of foul play at the house. Everything looked to be in perfect order. Suitcases still stored in the house, makeup still in the bathroom. Maid cleaned the place two days ago. The maid hadn't noticed anything strange."

"Well, something very strange was going on in the household. Someone must know about this couple."

Rutherford said, "The Beacon's liked to entertain a lot. There was a party last weekend."

"I need the guest list, delivery people, caterers, garden, pool, and anyone else that contacted the Beacons recently. I also want the financial information on the two subjects."

Simms looked strange. Derek said, "What is it?"

Simms responded, "Oh, I just remembered it's my visitation day to see my wife. She's in this nursing home and sometimes floats in and out of dementia."

Derek looked at his watch and said, "Sorry about that. We should be done in about fifteen minutes as the boys arrived to crack the safe open."

The house safe was opened, and it was totally empty. Derek said, "That was unusual. Okay, we're done here for now." Derek left to get ready for his date. He started whistling with the car radio music.

5   Dinner with Jess

HE PICKED JESS up from her hotel at seven o'clock sharp. She knew he would be punctual. Jess wore a soft flowing sundress with crisscrossed straps in a pale champagne color with matching sandals. She wore a gorgeous large gray pearl necklace with diamonds. Her perfume filled his senses. Her long blond hair was down except for a single side braid twisted to the back of her head with a gold barrette.

He was reminded of a flower. She was similar in color to a pale peony that grew in his mother's garden, soft and shimmery in the beautiful night. Where is that barrette going to land later?

Jess looked at Derek in casual slacks, soft knit shirt, and loafers. His handsome profile turned to look directly at her. Jess saw the "Hello, my sex kitten" look in Derek's eyes. Now Jess wished she selected her boring dark work pantsuit. She climbed into the sedan and sat down on the leather car seat.

This date might be a major mistake. They were so total opposites in lots of ways. The differences between them were miles and miles. He was into his way of doing things. Jess knew better ways. She needed space from Derek. She couldn't do this now. Her heart warred with her. The heart told her to go get him. She argued that she didn't have the time. Perhaps that was where the attraction came into play. She forgot there was massive heat between the two of them whenever they were in close quarters.

Jess wanted to discourage him. She tentatively asked, "How was your day, honey?"

Derek thought, *That's not good. She's sarcastic already*. He remembered her last voice message to him. This might have been a bad idea.

Derek pulled away from the hotel drive and waited until they were on the highway. They were headed to Pierre's in Yountville. It was an upscale restaurant, and he read the menu on their website. He remembered some of the food she liked. She also looked very nice. She smelled better than nice. Derek looked at Jess who glanced at him.

"I'm glad to escape work for one evening. Meeting you gave me the opportunity to leave early."

He wondered if some guy bought her the pearl necklace. It looked expensive and complemented her. Someone had very good taste. He hoped it wasn't that rich lawyer she dated a while ago.

"Thanks. You still haven't told me about your day. It must have been bad. I saw the dead body taken out of the jewelry store."

Half the people in town saw the covered body, so Derek said, "Yes, definitely a dead body."

This was going to take longer than she thought.

The meal was exquisite scallops and steak with tossed salad and baked potatoes. Jess knew it was great to eat good food. The little restaurant's menu across the Napa jewelry store was limited. Derek ordered one red sauvignon and a chardonnay bottle from their list of local wineries.

She told him about her book and finding the blueprints of an old winery location. She was excited about writing and enjoyed the experience. It was part of the art world. She believed she would be good at it. Jess was glad he was interested in easy topics. The evening hours went by fast. Both almost emptied those two bottles, getting carried away in funny stories about their childhoods. Jess's childhood was very calm compared to Derek's.

"My parents loved to travel and dragged my brother and I along for the ride. One time, they went to Rome and listened to this out-of-this-world tenor concert. I stored the song in my head and sung it for my mother the next day. She wanted to immediately enroll me in a highly prestigious musical school to fulfill her dream."

"Please you must sing the song for me. I love music, especially opera and symphonies. Pretty please."

"I can't right now, but someday in the shower, it would work." He had a twinkle in his eyes waiting for her response.

She needed to steer him away from those thoughts. He was flirting and toying with her. "What made you choose this profession?"

"I could wear a really big silver and pearl-handled gun with homemade bullets to catch them bad dude outlaws."

Jess groaned, "Oh, no, not a cowboy."

Derek was delighted he captured her attention. "Yes, major cowboy. I like to catch the bad guy, the con artist. It was the thing that challenges my brain. I feel good when they are locked away. The police's network and information databases were powerful tools available to me when I'm on a case. Everything works very well when we put all our facts and insights together. I want to contribute my talents there. Singing is a sideline bonus."

Jess grabbed more of that wine. She explained why she loved diamonds and worked in the jewelry store in downtown Los Angeles in the diamond district. Her stepmother never wore diamonds, and one day when she was younger, she became brave, used her babysitting money, and hopped on the bus downtown. One store displayed these beautiful clear stones that sparkled mightily. She knew she needed to have some. She wanted to touch them. Hence, she studied everything about the precious gem."

Their meal was over and only a few other couples were in the restaurant. "Do you need more air? We can drive further north. I really don't mind." Derek always enjoyed talking with her. It was a pleasurable evening sharing stories. He would like to do it again soon, as he would be in Napa for the rest of the week.

"No, it's getting late. I want to drive to Tomales Bay in the morning for bird shots. The herons come in the area this time of year. They'll be important photos I wouldn't want to miss."

The two of them left the restaurant. Derek was quiet on the drive back to her hotel room, letting the radio music fill in the space. He opened the sliding roof glass window to let in the cool evening air. Jess received no further information out of him during dinner.

She needed to learn more about her diamond necklace. Was the precious item still in the store?

Her decision was made. She reminded herself that she entered this date for a reason.

Walking to her room, Derek knew he couldn't get enough of Jess. He needed to figure out what to say to make her invite him inside. When they reached the door, Jess asked, "Do you like scotch?"

Derek smiled to himself. The gods were still working in his favor. There would be no lonely hotel room tonight. He hated scotch unless it was very old, but tonight he would drink anything to get in Jess's pants. He replied, "Absolutely, yes."

Jess wondered if she might be getting more than she bargained for. Derek could bring complications into the game. The two drinks were poured and probably two sips were taken. Derek touched Jess and enveloped her into his strong arms. She felt better than the flower. Her skin and hair softer than the small velvet petals.

He kissed her slowly, tender, and long. The fire and heat between their two bodies was immense, the pleasure centers hitting on target every time. Jess knew lovers before, but when they became serious, she would leave permanently. This Derek guy was an amazing fountain of all-night strength.

Jess turned loose her heightened desires and welcomed Derek with full passion. The electricity in the air melted the two hearts into one. The glorious night slid past them. They were lost to the world in their own private domain of easy loving.

The next morning, while he was in the shower, he sang opera. Jess smiled and liked his deep voice. A mother would love that voice. She went through all his pockets and found the note written by Bill Barker and read it. She sank into the chair. She knew her dream of retrieving her mother's necklace had been foiled. The beautiful diamond necklace was one of the items missing. Her heart broke into a million pieces. She was crest fallen and then angry.

Jess expounded, "Not her diamond necklace. Unbelievable bad luck."

She must regain her composure. Jess pulled up her determined strength and went into actress mode. Derek couldn't know.

Derek left the hotel to go back to the investigation. Everything seemed great with Jess. She told him she liked his shower song very much. They both arranged to meet for pizza at a place that served vegetarian and cooked the soft dough in special ovens. It was her treat. Derek was happy and wore a grin on his face.

"He needed to tone things down or people would wonder where he spent the night." She kissed him softly.

Derek didn't care what people thought at all. His personal life was his business.

He pulled Jess back into his arms. Derek gave Jess an awesome see-her-later kiss, a definitely-wonderful-later kiss, and maybe beyond-stratosphere-wonderful kiss.

Derek decided he could learn to like scotch. No problem for Derek to like anything Jess did.

He was clueless to the turmoil surrounding Jess. She always was good at covering her tracks when her world fell apart.

Jess learned to hide her feelings after her mother died as her father struggled. Looking forward to her day in Tomales Bay, she pulled her equipment together. Derek told her he loved oysters, and she would try to bring him some.

6   Body on the Shoreline

JESS WASN'T TIRED at all. It was early, so she drove to Tomales Bay with her camera for the bird shots. Her rental car was left on the small back road. She reminded herself that Tomales Bay sat on the submerged portion of the San Andreas Fault and was approximately a mile or so wide by approximately fifteen miles long. Traveling through the low water in her rubber boots, she saw some herons ahead and stopped for some photo shots. Checking the camera pictures, she was happy with them. She was surprised at the distance she walked. Her car was barely discernible.

Wanting a few more shots, she turned away from the trees and moved further into the water. She was carrying her lightweight lens and tripod in the backpack. Stopping to change lenses, she noticed her boots were sinking more into the muck. Jess knew she must move back to shallower water. She looked another direction and took a shot of a flock of birds flying toward the ocean. The picture was excellent.

Jess moved toward the shallower part of the water when she noticed a fallen tree in the water. Moving even closer, she stepped on a tree trunk and almost fell. Only it was not a tree trunk; it was a dead woman's body!

Who was the woman? How did the woman get here? Was the body here a long time? Frantic thoughts ran through her mind.

The body wasn't too bloated yet, so it was likely not too long in the water. Jess wanted to see if the body contained any identification and wondered if she should check the pockets. She decided she better not touch anything and leave her DNA on the body or the scene.

She moved back from the body and fished out Derek's business card. She almost dropped the card as she dug out her cell phone. Movement was hard. She felt cold suddenly. She hadn't noticed the cold before. It was better to call a friend than the local cops. She dialed, and he picked up on the first ring.

"Derek Wright here."

"I need some help in Tomales Bay. Can you come right away?" Jess almost dropped her phone in the marsh. She knew she was panicking.

Derek was up to his eyeballs with cops, neighbors, his superiors, and now the press. "Jess, we can talk tonight, unless you're hurt or something."

Jess blurted out, "It's that *something* word."

It was the way she said *something*, sort of in a shaky voice, that convinced him something was wrong. She was emotionally distraught. Feelings of dread touched Derek.

"The something was a dead body something, possibly female something."

Derek knew she was repeating words, "Where is she exactly? And don't touch anything."

"I stepped on the something and hadn't meant to do that at all," Jess said and then started crying.

"Oh, no, honey, don't cry. Just give me the coordinates so I can find you. Don't you still carry that terrific guidance device in your backpack? You can just turn the button on and read to me the numbers."

That stopped her crying immediately. How did Derek know about the guidance device in her backpack? The backpack was in the trunk of the locked rental car when they were together.

Jess dug it out and turned the alien object over. She turned on the device, gave him the coordinates, and hung up.

Panicking, she moved toward the roof of her car in the distance. It was the only thing she saw or heard. She knew she was afraid of what was out in the marshland. He tried to call her back, but she left the dead body and didn't answer. She freaked out and needed to throw up somewhere. Hastily placing her gear in the trunk, she also wanted some scotch. Driving toward the friendly restaurant bar she noticed before on the State 1 road, she parked in the space in front of the building. She exited her rental car. Safety existed within the bar.

XXXXXX

Derek asked, "How in the world did someone go to Tomales Bay and stumble upon a dead body?" It was giving him a creepy feeling and he didn't like it.

The local cops were notified and set things up to meet him there. He drove from Napa to Tomales Bay. Then he saw Jess's rental car by a restaurant bar and swerved into an empty street side parking spot. He walked into the bar and there she was with her black muddy rubber boots taken off. Her bare feet wrapped around the brass and wood bar stool as she was eating oysters and taking a sip of the drink. She looked relaxed in her camel color sweater and matching tight-knit pants. Her camel leather biker jacket was partially thrown over the chair. He had seen her field jacket that she wore in the marshland area in her car. Jess's hair was pulled out from her gold elastic band and cascaded down her back in curls. The hair band wrapped around her drink glass. She looked like a fashion plate in her designer clothes seated at the bar. Even when he saw her in blue jeans, she looked super good. For the moment, she acted like a tourist having a good time. No weeping woman was in this room.

Was the weeping woman an act? He even worried how much she had to drink?

Jess was blissfully happy and exuberantly glad to see him. She popped the last oyster in his mouth. Her hands were ice-cold.

"How much scotch?" The bartender held up three fingers, glad someone was getting the pretty lady out of the bar.

She must go to the bathroom. He waited and ushered her back into his sedan. Jess pointed out directions for him. He stopped the car and told her, "Stay in the vehicle. Don't open the windows and keep the doors locked. I'll be back as soon as I could get away."

He hiked a few short blocks and saw the technicians moving the body and cops talking. He hated to leave her, but he thought she would be fine. He walked to his second murdered body.

Meanwhile, Jess found paper and pencil and left Derek a note. She hated to wait there with the dead woman's body and must leave at once. She would drive her car back to her hotel.

It took Derek two hours at the scene. He went back to the car and read her note. Now he was pissed. He told her to wait, but she hadn't listened to him. It dawned on him that it was a mistake to leave her when she was extremely upset. He should have stayed with her.

7   Pizza with Jess

DEREK ARRIVED AT her hotel with the gourmet vegetarian takeout pizza and beer. Jess smiled and opened the door.

After they ate pizza, he took her hand. "Don't ever do that again. You scared me. What if the killer was still around watching everyone? You might have been in imminent danger. I couldn't protect you if you don't listen."

"I hadn't thought of that. Next time I would stay."

He looked at her and hoped there wasn't going to be a next time.

Jess needed to give her statement to the cops tomorrow. He explained to them she became ill, so they were okay. One of their cops also left when he was ill. The cop knew the victim and had major difficulty after the recognition of an old high school friend.

"Then they knew very well the dead woman's name."

Derek groaned because the day had been a long one, so he told her about the victim's small coin purse with her identification. "The victim was also shot in the head with what looked like a thirty-eight pistol. She was shot about fifty feet from where Jess found her. It appeared she might have crawled quite some ways before dying, and the water floated the body a little farther. It was the wife of the dead jeweler."

Jess's eyes became huge, and she said, "No way. Then either the husband or wife may have known their murderer."

Derek knew the weeping woman hadn't been an act. She was afraid encountering the body. Jess left the scene because she was afraid. What if she felt the killer nearby? Would she trust him enough to tell him?

"High probability the husband and wife both knew the killer. Did you feel something at the Tomales Bay scene that made you run? I don't want any small detail to go unnoticed."

"I'm not sure. I felt the situation was urgent, so I left. I don't quite know how to describe what I felt."

He was relieved. "People occasionally panic when they run into a dead body. I'm glad you're safe. Next time, I would have to handcuff you to the sedan."

Missing her when she left Tomales Bay, he grabbed her and locked her hands with his. Then he released her hands. She saw the thunder and desire in his eyes. He started kissing her all over. Jess was delighted he shared information. She didn't know the police would be releasing a statement that evening to warn people to lock doors and be on the lookout for suspicious activity. The dead woman's identity would be revealed.

Derek and Jess made more passionate love. Derek ate the rest of the pizza because he hadn't eaten but a small bite of the oysters earlier. Jess forgot about buying him some in her haste to leave. She wrapped her feet around his body, driving him crazy with lustful thoughts. He put those thoughts into action. Then more longer and slower love with Jess. They were both exhausted and fell asleep in each other's arms until morning.

Before Derek left to go back to the investigation, he asked her a question. "How long is your vacation?"

"I'm registered for only a week at this hotel."

"Don't you ever answer a question straight?"

Jess replied, "Two weeks."

It was a good thing she told him the truth because he called her work office and already checked. He also checked her rental vehicle out when she was in the shower. He figured out how to get into her notebook computer but couldn't understand any of her notes. He even looked at the pictures on her digital camera. There were just pictures of the beach and some of Tomales Bay. He would have to convince her to stay with him at his hotel in town.

Tomorrow he would meet with his superiors about some more information he received. The information was something to do with the two-hundred-fifty-thousand-dollar diamond necklace. Derek worried about how many people knew about the necklace and why people wanted that very particular item. Evidently, there was a necklace that belonged to an elderly woman in Los Angeles. She claimed that she knew royal blood and that her necklace once belonged to royalty. The elderly lady's neighbors never believed her. Her own adopted son didn't even believe her.

The elderly woman's son brought the necklace to this specific jeweler's shop in Napa while she was on vacation for cleaning and repair on the end clasp. The adopted son went to the jeweler to pick up the necklace and brought it back home. The adopted son decided to first have it appraised at a different jeweler and found out the necklace was paste glass.

If the jeweler in Napa made the switch on the elderly lady, then it would be a whole new ball game. The police knew that the elderly lady was supposed to have died from a heart attack after her adopted son brought home the necklace from the jeweler's, but the autopsy completed was a poison compound. The police had taken a photograph of the woman holding a necklace. The clasp was clearly visible.

Three unsolved murders made his superiors anxious to catch the criminals and wrap up the case.

The adopted son tried to find the paste copy of the necklace after the funeral, and it seemed to have disappeared. He hadn't filed a report with the police because that necklace was not worth very much. If the original diamond necklace was old and from royalty, then it was probably worth more money than thought.

Out of all the jewelry in the store, there was no insurance placed upon the necklace nor any picture. All the jewels over three thousand dollars in this shop had been photographed and were insured in case of fire or burglary.

Simms called and said, "The autopsy report confirmed her death was because of the bullet. The wife's body contained semen inside. The semen was not her husband's, so the lover theory was more than likely a correct one. The potential killer was the lover. I wonder if someone saw the two people together. If the lovers were careful, then perhaps no one knew about it."

Derek replied, "The jewelry store manager and his wife were part of the con artist game. Their financials showed they were heavily in debt. Stealing jewelry and then selling the jewelry in their store was a perfect setup. Unfortunately for the police, the lover killer was out in the world together with a possible fourth one, the poisoner. Besides those two, there probably existed more accomplices."

He thought Derek was absolutely-right-on with those theories. Simms hated to think the murderers were still hanging around his town. He would notify his people to maintain high vigilance for any suspicious activity. He didn't need any more of the dead bodies.

8   Jess and the Cops

FOR SOME REASON, cops made Jess nervous. She knew it was because of the necklace. It was two years since the elderly woman brought it into the very small jewelry shop in Los Angeles where Jess worked. She was the only one in the shop that early morning. The elderly woman banged on the glass door of the shop, holding the necklace up to the glass, so Jess let her in. Jess examined the necklace and knew it was legitimate. She had gotten the elderly woman's name and address and phone.

The elderly woman told her the story about the necklace. The necklace was a gift given to her from royalty. She saved their child when they were on vacation in Italy. The child almost drowned. The elderly woman really stole the necklace from her dead neighbor who died in a car accident, but she didn't tell anyone that part. She wanted that necklace and took it the day of the funeral. The story was the dead friend's story, only the elderly lady made the story her own.

"Can I take a picture of the necklace? I could do some research as to the necklace's worth? The design is unusual and older. I'll give you an insurance estimate of value for the forty-six-carat diamond necklace at approximately two hundred forty-five thousand dollars now. The actual worth could be more than that. Any additional information could be mailed to you."

The woman became agitated. "No pictures. You cannot do that. There won't be any pictures. It is trouble."

She put the necklace in her purse and raced out of the shop and disappeared. When Jess could get vacation from work, she drove to the woman's house and saw it was empty and condemned. The only thing the neighbors knew was her adopted son finally picked her up and left with her. They knew no forwarding address, so Jess tried finding her on the computer, but to no avail. Then one day, she saw the necklace in the Napa shop.

The diamond necklace was the same. The story was her mother's story. That's exactly when she went into action to figure out a way to steal the necklace.

She learned about safes and alarm systems, cameras, and breaking into and out of buildings. Then she found another job working for a larger jeweler that owned the same type of safe as the Napa Jewelry store. Jess practiced and practiced unlocking the safe.

It was during this period when she met Derek Wright from Los Angeles. They went out on two dates, so she decided to follow him one day. He told her that he was in marketing but wouldn't tell her where specifically he worked. He created some crazy story about a berserk college girlfriend who tried to kill him once. He wouldn't tell her any more of the girlfriend story, so he never told girls where he worked or for what company.

When she found out he was a major investigator in his own firm who worked with police, she dropped him. She told him she wasn't his type and she moved on. She did it via a phone call message the day after she moved and changed jobs. She knew he could find her, but thought those two things would send a strong message. And she was here again with Derek, only now she did need his help to find the location of the special diamond necklace.

Jess entered the police station. She understood Derek was in a meeting today but didn't know anything about it. She provided the gruesome details about finding the woman's body. The police provided her with no information. She was going to have to watch the news again just to find out what was happening with the investigation. She selected coffee out of the machine with cream.

Officer Simms was waiting behind her and smiled. "I saw the man who loaded the coffee machine. The bag stated the contents were coffee, but the final brewed stuff was real terrible. You might want to rethink drinking that poison."

Jess's eyes grew bigger, "What an odd thing to say? At least it was wet and hot, just what I needed today."

"How did you know where to find a dead body?"

"I didn't. It was just something I accidentally stepped on."

Simms squinted his eyes and said, "Yeah, right." Simms walked away.

Jess drove back to her hotel. Her room was trashed, and clothes were thrown everywhere. She ran down to the office, where the manager walked with her back to the room. The manager was glad nothing was broken; he could call the police.

"No, I will call my Los Angeles investigator friend, who's very good at this kind of strange happening."

XXXXXX

Derek was still in his meeting, so Jess left him a voice-mail on his cell phone. Derek saw Jess's number on the voice-mail but must stay in his meeting. When he picked up the message, he almost ran down Simms who was close to their conference room door.

He got in his vehicle and hit the button for the lights and siren. Jess heard him coming and was standing outside her room with her gear, backpack, and suitcase in hand.

"She is not staying here at this hotel. Who would do such a thing? She needs a warm body next to her with a big gun."

This spelled trouble for Jess. Someone didn't want her in Napa. He was glad she packed. She could stay with him.

38

Derek looked at the room and talked to the hotel manager. Derek called the local cop and explained the situation. The local cop would handle the break-in incidence. Taking Jess back to his hotel room a few days earlier than planned, he was happy to share his bed with her. She packed all her stuff into his sedan. They would pick up her rental car later.

9   Pool Boy's Nosy Friend

THE MURDERER WAS looking for the pool boy. The pool boy saw the murderer with Mrs. Beacon of the jeweler's house. The murderer was messing around with the wife during the day, getting some extra action in his life. The wife helped him with information, so he would get rid of her husband. The murderer's girlfriend didn't know about their relationship.

The pool boy was a surfer kid who went for two weeks south to the beaches around Los Angeles. The murderer asked the boy's employer about his whereabouts, and the employer knew nothing. His mom wasn't home because she went to visit her sister.

The murderer questioned all over the streets of Napa and finally hit pay dirt. Some friends knew he went to the Manhattan Beach area. The murderer talked to pool boy's friend, Mark. The murderer went to the Los Angeles surf areas searching for the pool boy. He was nowhere to be found.

He carried no cell phone with which to locate him. It was as if he vanished into thin air. The murderer drove back to Napa and waited. The murderer worked on a plan to dispose of pool boy and anyone else that got in the way. The necklace was safely hidden for now.

Pool boy met a new girlfriend who was into horses. He knew nothing about horses. Despite that fact, she invited him to stay as a horse boy on her parent's estate. He didn't care if he ever went back to Napa. The girlfriend showed him all the other cool beaches closer to her parent's home in San Diego. So, the pool boy was in heaven traversing both the surf and horse worlds with his newfound best friend. Along the way, pool boy made new friends, so he quickly forgot his old friends.

Mark was one of those curious boys who always did stupid things. Mark had no clue he was messing with evil. He didn't like the person who asked him questions about his friend, pool boy. He believed that something was up, so he started following that person.

Snooping around pool boy's place of work, the Beacons' house, Mark hoped to find some clues. He knew pool boy buried some of his money on the property, so his mom didn't know how much he made. Pool boy's mom always wanted more money from the kid. It didn't take long for the murderer to catch on to the happenings of Mark.

The murderer let Mark dig up the lawn for a few days until the murderer had set up the trap. Mark was excited because today he was following the person down Shady Lane and into the woods. Mark took another road, Spruce Lane, and parked his car. He left the car, walked through the woods so he could sneak up on the person. The Shady Lane road reached a dead-end because a lot of trees blocked the end portion of the road.

Now the murderer knew the Department of Roads removed the dead trees and the road was reopened. When Mark came through the woods, there sat the murderer in the car in the cleared road. Mark thought there was no problem. He was safe. So, he came closer to the murderer who stepped out of the car. The next thing Mark saw was the gun. Pool boy had asked Mark to go with him to the beach. Mark didn't go because he thought surfing was hard work. He knew that was a bad decision—a very bad one.

XXXXXX

Derek received the call on his radio. It was Simms. "Some turkey hunters found a dead body, a young man's dead body in the woods off Shady Lane. The body showed one bullet hole to the head."

"No witnesses and massive tire tracks, footprints, and trash in the area from the workers who cleared the road. The body belonged to a Mark Jones. He was a friend of pool boy."

"Let's visit the parents for information."

The police also tried to find pool boy who disappeared. Even pool boy's mother didn't know where he was. Obviously, there was some connection with the two boys and the murderer.

Derek and Simms went to talk to the boy's parents. The parents didn't know anything or the reason their kid had a shovel in the trunk of his car. They did search his room and found a newer photo of pool boy that might help. Derek's superiors were upset at the third murder in Napa. This was the fourth murder counting the Los Angeles poisoning. Derek needed to catch this con artist and soon.

10   Calling a Friend for Help

DEREK TUCKED JESS safely in for the night. They drove earlier to Yountville and ate at a heavenly pasta sauce restaurant. There was a combination of pasta dish with different sauces. The menu contained a total of twelve sauces and they chose six different sauces. They ate the pasta off one large platter and shared the delectable dishes. Jess stabbed Derek gently with her fork when he kept eating her vegetarian sauce.

After dinner, they came home and made love. Derek brought two of the forks home and was gently touching her skin on her tummy with them. She told him he had better send those forks back or she would tell Simms. He took out his handcuffs and told her she should be careful. She gleefully succumbed to him with her hands held out, daring him. He pulled her closer throwing the cuffs on the floor. The sex was so hot that he was still zoning in and out from the experience. They both felt melted again inside, electricity fully ramped to high; it was better than any night rock show.

He stepped out of their room and called his old friend, a former detective in another area of the big Southern city in California. His friend retired to take care of his wife when she developed cancer. His wife was gone now, and he did freelance work. Jim Michaels was available and would be on the next airplane out. Derek needed a friend to guard Jess when he was busy with the investigation.

Derek had been watching over Jess ever since she dumped him. He could now understand that berserk college girlfriend whom he dated in the past. He became obsessed with Jess and found out her new address and her new employer. He knew the places she ran and the gyms she frequented. He didn't understand some of the places or classes she attended. He saw her only a few times with men. She quickly dumped them also. He tried to figure her out and gave up.

Derek called her work and found out when she was going on vacation. His secretary called and found out about the Napa trip. He planned to accidentally run into her while she was jogging one day. Then the murder happened, which allowed a perfect entrance back into her life. He knew he was a goner. He wanted only her.

So now he must protect Jess. Someone got too close when they trashed her room. Derek swore that he was going to take that murderer down. Jess told him about the conversation with Simms. He checked out Simms record and the guy seemed just fine.

He couldn't tell Jess how he felt. He tried that on date number two, but she ran. He couldn't blame her. He just realized his mistake too late. Derek learned his lesson and was going to try to play the game of love better this time.

Derek held back his private thoughts about their future together. He saw them living together married. If she knew he even tracked her, Jess would run again for real. He knew then he wouldn't find her. He talked a lot about Jess to his friend, Jim, so there was no need for further explanation to the protector guy. Jim would do the job well. Having been around so long, Jim trusted no one and figured that was why he was still alive.

Derek saw the jewelry store videos taken during the day from the supposed hidden camera. The cameras inside the store were turned off at night. "Stupid move by the store manager."

He recognized Jess inside the store immediately, and the police video guy backed up and replayed the scene slower several times. She kept her face down always, letting the bill portion of the cap cover her face.

"It was almost as if she knew where the camera was in that store. She looked at some sixteen thousand-dollar necklaces."

Bill Barker confirmed it was Jess inside the store and the price range of the necklaces. Bill told Derek about the Fancy Violet Gray small diamond necklace that attracted her attention. Derek knew that colored stone was her mist that appeared in her photos. Derek thought it odd that she hadn't mentioned that important fact to him--the fact that she was in the jewelry store several times.

Derek said to the video guy, "Stop, right there. Move a second and stop. Do it again."

There was a slight turn of her head as she looked toward the two-hundred-fifty-thousand-dollar necklace. Bill was turned away from Jess. He was talking to another clerk in the store, so he hadn't seen the slight turn toward that expensive locked case. Then Jess stepped backward a few paces and turned while tilting her head, so it was hard to see her profile. Derek noticed all her body movements in the video.

"She was almost in stealth mode, not your typical, average tourist in a store."

Bill had given an accurate enough description of the necklace so that a drawing was made for the police. Bill said the clasp on the drawing wasn't right, and he couldn't remember it exactly.

Did Jess see the necklace clasp? Women remember details better. Derek would have to ask her. He would have to ask her very carefully as he suddenly remembered her high-powered night vision binoculars in the trunk of her locked car. Did women really buy those things? Now he was surprised there wasn't a gun.

11   Arrival of Detective Friend

DEREK TOLD NO one about his hired friend. Derek also trusted no one. Jim Michaels checked his camera gear, backpack, tripod, water bottle, tourist clothes, old fishing hat, fly rod and reel, and revolver. The rifle was also in the trunk with the high-powered scope as were the knives, bow and arrow, and several hunting permits. There were night vision goggles, a handheld guidance system device, climbing shoes, ropes, and gear. He had the works in that trunk.

If anyone asked, he'd tell them they were renovating his garage and that he used his vehicle to currently store stuff. He could hardly wait for the workers to get done with the larger garage. He was staying at the same hotel as Derek and Jess.

The first morning there, he got up early to follow Jess in his rental car. Derek told him she was headed to Point Reyes for an early morning photo shoot, wanting to arrive when the park opened. Jim had Derek pick up some sandwiches the night before from this shop he drove by in Napa. They made their own buns and the smell had driven him crazy. He kept the sandwiches in the hotel room small refrigerator, not knowing how long a day at the beach would take. Jess did have to get back by three in the afternoon to Napa to meet with the police sketch artist person.

She confirmed to Derek that she saw the pretty necklace while in the store. It was hard to miss with the high number of overhead lights. She would be glad to help the police.

Jess needed to get out of Napa after hearing about that young man's death. It brought back visions of the dead woman's body. She loved going to Point Reyes and knew it would be a good photo shoot. It was a site she included in her vacation plans. Any opportunity to hit a beach anywhere in the country was always a point of interest. She began selling her photos to a gallery in Los Angeles, and her photos of the beach were great sellers.

Rain was predicted later in the evening. She wished she didn't have the police appointment because she also liked the storm cloud photos. Oh, well, there would be a next time.

On the drive, she rationalized about how Derek brought up the jewelry store video images of her. He went to this sandwich shop and came back to their room with huge sandwiches stuffed full of various kinds of meat. He had the tomatoes, lettuce, and pickles wrapped in a separate bag along with the foil-wrapped condiments. There were two extra-large sandwiches, chips, and a large bottle of wine from the next-door shop. The quantity of food was enough for her to take a sandwich on her hike to Point Reyes. He also picked up some water and orange juice in bottles.

After eating the sandwiches, she tickled his feet and they made tickled love in lots of other places. When she was satiated in complete bliss state, he brought up the videos. It was good distraction techniques at work.

Meanwhile, on the drive, Jim was following Jess's vehicle when he noticed another vehicle following the two of them. Jim pulled over to let the other car go past. The car was driven by a cop from Napa. Jim pulled back onto the road following both vehicles. He remembered the three tracking devices he brought with him that could be attached to a person's vehicle. After about twenty miles, the Napa car turned around and headed back to Napa.

"Very odd tail. I wrote down the license number. I should give the information to Derek as twenty miles was too far outside our jurisdiction."

Jess pulled into the Point Reyes campground, and Jim pulled over way behind her. He waited for five minutes, giving her time to get a little ahead of him on the trail. It was early, and he hadn't seen any tourists on the small road. The tourists usually didn't appear until ten in the morning because they always ate the free breakfast before heading out sightseeing with the children.

Jim took his camera gear out of the trunk and put water bottle and sandwiches in the bag along with bullets and revolver. He put a tracking device on Jess's rental car. He next put on his favorite hat and windbreaker and walked up the pathway towards the landmark lighthouse and Jess.

She was taking fantastic shots of the lighthouse this morning as there were fine wispy clouds in the distance. Partial shots included the huge expanse of beach three hundred feet below. After half an hour, she noticed the other few tourists, as the mass had not yet arrived.

There was the old guy from their Napa hotel, and Jess recognized his hat, a very distinctive used fishing hat. Jess also noticed he ate the same type of sandwich she and Derek decimated last night. The wrapper was the same store.

Jim saw Jess looking at his sandwich and wished he had eaten the sandwich on the drive to Point Reyes. Derek told him that Jess was smart and to not under estimate her. Jim put the last bite in his mouth and stashed the wrapper in a pocket of his backpack.

He stood up and introduced himself. "I'm Jim Michaels from Los Angeles. I like your camera very much. Mine is an older version. Watching you take pictures from strategic locations is a pure pleasure. The weather today is perfect. Don't you think so, too?"

Then he started talking lenses, tripod, other cameras, photo shots, and galleries with Jess to distract her. Jess invited Jim to move along with her with his camera. They finished shooting photos of Point Reyes together, moving to the best cliff places with a few seagulls floating on the air. Jess checked her watch. It was time to leave.

Jess saw the bakery on the drive over. It advertised homemade rolls and spinach quiche. The bakery also sold local wine. She mentioned the bakery to Jim. He also saw the wonderful store. The two of them agreed to stop there and pick up their favorite food on the way to Napa. Jess was going to bring some food back to the hotel for Derek and her dinner.

The two stopped at the chef-owned bakery that sold out of the quiche but had some that were frozen. The bakery told them the quiches would work well in the microwave. They just needed to go slow. It was important that they didn't overcook the eggs. Jim picked the Ham and Swiss quiche.

Driving back to Napa, Jim waved to Jess as she was headed toward the police station. Then he turned in the driveway of the hotel. He reached his room and caught a nap, having safely deposited Jess with police and later Derek. Jim remembered his wife. *Lucky Derek*, he thought, as he got to know a little more about Jess today. Jim liked Jess; she reminded him of good times.

12 Diamond Necklace Clasp

NOW JESS MUST divulge information about the clasp. She shouldn't provide all the information that clasp told, not at this juncture anyway. She met with the police sketch artist who showed her Bill's drawing. They pulled up the sketch on the computer and the artist listened to Jess's description.

She corrected the artist sketch to the number of diamonds as there were four small additional stones on each side in a circular setting like a little globe right before the clasp. Describing to him the millimeter description and shapes in the clasp, she also explained the location of a special ridge of twist on the top in the platinum metal. The description of the placement and size of each diamond in the clasp was given to him as well.

She didn't give the police sketch person the inscription information that was inside the one-inch clasp nor any other facts. The elderly woman showed Jess how to open the clasp to view the inside inscription. The inside inscription was addressed, "To Sami."

Jess's real mother was called Samantha. Jess called her mother Sami. It took a very thin jeweler's tool and a person was needed to touch the correct location to access the release.

The special outside twist on the top of the clasp was the clue that wasn't replicated on the paste necklace. The elderly woman couldn't see very well, but she lovingly touched that clasp over and over from the day she stole it. Some nice person brought the elderly woman a basket of tea and cookies. It was right before her adopted son brought back the necklace from the jewelers.

The elderly woman had drunk some tea and ate cookies while she waited for her adopted son. When the elderly woman touched the returned necklace, she moved to the clasp and knowledge came across her face. The necklace was a fake because the ridge of twist was gone. The elderly woman tried to stand up and speak, but she couldn't get any words out. The poison had overtaken her body at that point.

The murderer was home and removed the diamond necklace from its hiding place. The murderer held the necklace to the light and watched the perfectly matched stones sparkle into glints of light, holding a person mesmerized by their beauty. The murderer was happy. Everyone was stupid. The murderer won the con artist game because no one knew who stole the jewelry or why.

The murderer looked back at the deaths and felt stronger, more powerful than ever. The psychopathic mind was worsening every day. The psycho looked at the necklace three times and now there were three people shot dead.

The murderer knew the necklace must be sold. The murderer started looking for a fence, someone to sell the necklace. The murderer knew people who knew people. The murderer started the phone calls.

Derek went back to the hotel. He couldn't get the sketches out of his brain.

"I saw the new police artist sketches and was totally blown away. There was also a side view of the clasp. How could Jess have seen that much in the three videos of about ten seconds' total when she glanced toward the case? Was it photographic memory? It was those globe things; how could she see all the diamonds."

"Or did she assume the diamonds were all around the balls? Then some ridged twist, where did she see that under the very secure, locked glass case? Well, I hadn't seen the necklace, so I would have to check back with Bill, the jewelry sales clerk, on the drawing in the morning. Then I can re-release the artist's sketch to the police."

He was tired, but stopped at Jim Michaels' room for an update.

"Jess Jameson is a talented photographer and an all-around, super nice, intelligent, conversational woman. But that is just the start, I noticed how dreamy pretty she is."

Derek was in no mood and asked Jim, "What else?"

Jim rested, and even went down to the hotel bar and met this nice retired schoolteacher from Los Angeles. Jim invited her to dinner and was in a good mood. His friend, however, was slightly off. *Perfectly understandable* thought Jim. Between the investigation and Jess, the boy was tied up in knots. It was a rock and a hard place to be.

"She noticed my sandwich and the wrapper."

"Oh, no."

Jim was frowning.

"There was more, wasn't there?"

Jim told him about the local female cop that tailed Jess. Derek looked at Jim and they both knew, "More trouble. There should be no tail on Jess. She came here to take photos while on vacation. Moreover, Simms would have informed him."

"I thought the cop tracking Jess was odd. Do you want another tail on the cop car?"

"Yes, let's see what becomes of the unknown tail."

Derek rode the elevator to their room. When he stepped inside, there was Jess with chilled wine, warm rolls, warm quiche, and barely anything on. Derek saw very, very warm body. Suddenly, energy was rocking in his veins, and he was no longer tired. Derek was glad. as he was in no mood to leave this room.

Jess waited until Derek had eaten and drunk wine, and they made love several times. When he was satiated in complete bliss state and almost asleep, she brought up the tails.

Jess thought, *Distraction technique on perfect overdrive.*

"I know the one tail. It was the nice Jim Michaels person at your hotel. Is he a friend of yours? Who was the other tail?" she said.

Derek was wide awake, knowing full well it was going to be an hour before he could sleep. He was thinking fifteen minutes to explain and then forty-five minutes of makeup sex. Makeup sex was always good. After ten minutes of explaining to Jess, he stopped.

She totally got it. She had forgiven him. He thought of the five extra more minutes plus the hot forty-five minutes, and then he could forget the world. Derek would get some very much needed sleep.

13   The Fence Set Up

THE PROBLEM WITH fences of illegal goods was that all the fences know each other. It was an underground, underworld business with closely guarded secrets, alliances, and clients. The police were never clients. Therefore, the murderer must go through a fence and found the process complicated.

While any fence that did happen to fall in contact with the psycho murderer, those fences would tragically die later after the transaction was completed. The fences knew the psycho person, so they tried to avoid these types of con artist transactions. There were always the newbie fences who weren't very smart. They became victims of the con artist and were really conned out of the game permanently.

Now Jess knew a fence of illegal goods. She met him one day at the manufacturer's Safe class. It was the same manufacturer of the safe that her jewelry store kept on their premises. The store thought she should learn all about the safe when one day she showed massive interest in how the safe worked, what it was constructed of, how the locks worked, etc. They paid for her class.

The fence was this elderly gentleman in finely dressed clothes. She liked his shoes. He told her Italians made the best shoes.

Jess was the one who presented a problem to him. "If a person knew a person who somehow magically obtained something that they needed to sell, but couldn't quite do so in the open market, how would a person do such a thing?"

He looked at Jess and thought *the woman is not stupid at all*.

He invited her to have dinner in San Francisco with him, and she accepted. He liked her and gave her his private business card if she ever needed a small favor in the future. She was free to contact him any time at all. Jess reminded him of someone.

She said the word, *magical*. "I don't know but one woman who talked that way. You obviously are going to need my help. I would be glad to go there with you. I put your phone number under special client."

The murderer made his contact with the newbie fence. The murderer knew the older fences and placed a call to them. The older fence guys declined. The old guys knew there was this stolen necklace out there supposedly from royalty. None of the old guys believed that story at all about royalty. It was the oldest line in the book of fences. They did believe the necklace was stolen, just like 85 percent of their transactions.

The newbies didn't care about royalty and only heard the word *diamonds*. Diamonds meant money. The older fences, except one, all laughed. He heard a partial story from the magical girl named Jess. He believed the fence request was real, but wasn't going to touch it.

Dean was, however, going to let Jess know about the upcoming transaction. He made the phone call to Jess the next morning.

Jess recognized the number and picked up the call. Derek was thankfully in the shower. Jess knew that the murderer was going to try to get rid of the necklace. She called Dean about the necklace. She wanted to purchase the diamond necklace.

Her fence realized Jess could get into trouble. "If you want to view the transaction, I could possibly get involved to set everything up. I would do that scenario if you need me to."

Jess thanked her old friend, and before she hung up, she told him to wait for her call.

Derek stepped out of the shower when Jess entered the bathroom and she held the towel out of his range. He grabbed her and turned the shower back on. He lifted Jess back into the shower in her thin robe, stripping her of the wet garment. He took the water wand and sprayed her until she fell into his arms. Making love to her in the early morning hours with water silently cascading their young bodies, he gave her his strong love.

Derek was last out of the shower. Jess wrapped her towel around her. Turning around with a happy face, he had no clue what transpired before their joint shower.

After Derek left, she called back her friend, Dean Crain, "Set up the con artist fence meeting. I need to attend as a hidden person."

14   Pool Boy Found

THE LOS ANGELES people found pool boy with the new photo and put him into protective police custody until the girlfriend's father found out. The girl's father pulled pool boy out of their clutches so fast that time stood still. He contacted his entire team of legally very sharp lawyers. He golfed daily with the owner of the legal firm at this very prestigious golf course in San Diego.

His daughter was the apple of his eye. Whatever she wanted, it was hers, no questions asked. He liked the pool boy kid. He conversed with him about earning money. The kid was smart. The father of the girl even offered him a job in his wonderful company.

The only information that reached Derek on pool boy was, "Found wrong kid."

Derek flew to Los Angeles anyway. He had been around the block once or twice. He left Napa believing Jess was in Jim's capable hands.

Derek landed in San Diego, obtained a rental car, and headed toward the police station.

He received a call from Jim. "Jess checked out and left the hotel and was driving toward San Francisco."

"Why did she leave? She told me she was going to await my return. Follow her forever. Get back with me tonight or sooner if needed."

Jim knew boyfriend was freaking out on Jess's strange move. Jim was also freaking out. He had to leave that sexy, retired schoolteacher he ate dinner with in Napa the previous evening. "Where was Jess headed? What is in San Francisco?"

Jess turned the corner. A large truck was between them. Jim hit the truck and was forced to drop the tail because he couldn't get around the vehicle.

Only her fence knew about the meeting.

Derek received the address of the father and ran into perfect daughter and surfer boyfriend on the private road to the girl's home. Derek told surfer boy, i.e. pool boy about his friend Mark's murder and recommended immediate disappearance. He handed the pool boy his card and asked him to think back on any pool cleanings at the Beacon house and to let him know anything that came to mind. Derek told him, "Just leave a message."

Pool boy agreed. They went home, and the girl's father had his daughter and pool boy on a cruise ship to Europe, heavily guarded. Her father knew they wanted to get married in Greece and he put his team of lawyers on it to get everything ready. His wife was delighted to visit her family again in the close future.

The fences of all fences met and talked in San Francisco. Jess was hidden from the other fence's view.

It was all about price and market value and royalty. Nothing on price was agreed or confirmed. The necklace and murderer were fully cloaked in a layer of dishonest people wanting a piece of the green money prize. Dean knew it was the slowest, stupidest, most dumb-witted fence meeting he ever attended. Clearly, the person on the other end was either a cop or some idiot to hire such dim-wit, newbies. It was just a discussion meeting. The other fence didn't even bring the necklace. A new meeting would have to be set up.

So, her fence, Dean Crain, headed back home to his San Francisco condo.

Jess drove back to Napa to get her precious tools. Unfortunately for Jess, she drove by a cop car driven by the same female who tailed her earlier.

15   Thief's Tools

JESS WAS FOLLOWED by the cop lady, Sally Rutherford, into the wooded road. Stopping near a very large oak tree where she buried the jewelry store blueprints and her tools, she picked up the gear, which could be construed as extensive in the thievery world. By buried, not really, it was just a large pile of leaves. She was experienced in how to handle every piece of tool and gear in that package.

Rutherford followed Jess's car knowing her behavior over the past forty-eight hours were recorded by her as strange, and thief-like. Rutherford only followed Jess out of curiosity because she thought Jess was stupid. But then she saw all females as stupid. Men were even stupider.

Jess and Rutherford were followed at a distance by Jim Michaels who knew it was a very long day. He stepped out of his hidden car with his revolver and snuck upon the two women who were now in conversation. He saw the pile of leaves by the blueprints and tools. He knew to step back out of site and listen.

Rutherford held up high the blueprints and stated, "Lookey, what we have here. Girl, you're a piece of very dead meat. I'm taking you back to jail and you're never getting out."

"That's absurd. I've done nothing illegal. You're just overreacting to my items. I was only retrieving my equipment because I couldn't carry them when I incurred a bad muscle spasm. You can check that out with Derek Wright who saw me holding my side."

"I don't need to check with Mr. Wright. This is my territory. You're a stranger in town who clearly committed robbery and murder. The blueprints are the key. Where did you

59

stash the jewelry? I know you're guilty. You killed those three people and trashed your pistol somewhere. The police will find your gun which is probably in this same area. I'm done talking with you. Jess Jameson, you're under arrest for robbery and murder."

As Rutherford was handcuffing Jess, she laughed. That laugh sent chills up Jim's spine. Something was off. Jim followed Rutherford until Jess was placed safely in the local jail cell.

Jim slowly dialed the number for Derek, knowing full well the firestorm that was about to descend.

Derek picked up the call from Jim.

Jim was talking slow, and it was driving Derek nuts.

"Spill it, Jim. If something's wrong, you need to tell me. It's Jess, right? Where's Jess now?"

He explained every minute of what first happened and how he lost her tail for a little while in San Francisco after hitting a truck but picked it up while in Napa. Then there was the high-tech equipment and jewelry store building drawings Rutherford caught her retrieving in the woods. He hated to tell him where Rutherford clearly took Jess, thinking the worst of the situation. He included who said what between Rutherford and Jess plus the entire order of the conversation and time of day.

Jim was still talking when he realized Derek was no longer there. Derek was headed to the next airplane out of San Diego, burning rubber on that rental car. He didn't even wait for his rental car receipt, barely catching the plane that waited for him. He drove his next rental car to the Napa jail cell.

16   Jess in Jail

IT WAS SOMETIME after one in the morning, and Jess was still awake. She called her friend, Dean Crain, and replayed the night's happenings with the female Napa policewoman. She was in jail and needed help. She postponed calling her lawyer, Harv. She could do that in the morning.

She was told there was a visitor to see her. Jess thought, *weren't visiting hours over?*

It was Simms letting Derek into her cell. Derek was someone she didn't want to see yet and she complained to Simms. Simms just walked away and left Jess alone with Derek in her locked jail cell.

Derek slowly moved to the empty bunk bed and sat down. He looked at Jess. She saw heartbreak in his eyes and her body stiffened.

Derek recognized her defensive move. He saw it before. Derek sighed and relaxed. He was not her enemy, but the system would be shortly.

"Jess, talk to me please. No more locking me outside. You need to try to trust me. I'm more than a friend. You know how much more, or our nights together wouldn't have mattered. If those didn't matter, then you need to trust my professional experience."

"Sorry, but I can't involve you in this."

"Yes, you can. I'm here all the way, entire journey, every little thing. I'm not sorry about ever meeting you."

"I don't want any more people to get hurt. Your relationship with me would not help your reputation. It's too late. You should leave."

"I'm a smart guy and can take care of myself. By the way, I'm staying."

"There's a murderer on the loose. No, there are multiple murderers on the loose."

"Jess, let's combine forces and catch the creeps together."

Jess crossed the other side of the room slowly extending her hand. Derek held out both hands, and she went into Derek's open arms. "Didn't you realize I would be here?"

He stayed all night with her. Jess gave him a note for her friend, Dean Crain, so that her fence could set up the next meeting. The words were, "Run silent, run deep, lock everything down, do it magically."

The fence knew what those words meant when Derek found and approached him with Jess's note. The fence recognized her heart message at the end of the sentence. Jess taught the new fence her code. It became their code that existed between just the two of them from their meeting at the Safe class.

The meeting was between Derek Wright and Jess's fence, Dean Crain, with the police tuning in. The fence wrote something on a napkin that he handed to Derek. It was a harbor and dock number. Derek shook his head once.

Derek met Dean on the fence's very nice seventy-five-foot sailboat in Oakland harbor, and they sailed away into the sun. Jim was on the dock under disguise and was told to call the cops in four hours if Derek didn't return.

The sailboat glided with the wind under an able captain and crew. The weather was a beautiful day for freedom and for let's-forget-the-world sailing.

Derek remembered his night with Jess in jail, and a pained expression appeared on his face. The fence saw that look, and he and Derek went below, out of everyone's hearing range.

"Nice boat."

"Let's cut the crap and help Jess. My name's Dean Crain. And you look extremely familiar."

"You know my name from Jess," said Derek.

"No, you were that guy sitting in the car at the small urban airport when I picked up Jess for a date and flew her to San Francisco a few months back. You were tailing her. Boy, you must have it bad."

Derek started to say, "Don't tell."

Dean interrupted him, "No, I won't, but now you owe me a favor."

"All right, as long as the favor is legal."

Dean said, "Of course."

That was exactly what Derek wanted to hear. "Do you know Jess well?"

The fence ignored Derek and said, "Let's set up the thing so Jess doesn't have to spend another day in jail due to this con artist psycho killer."

"Jess told you about the killer?"

"Why do you think I'm here, for my health?"

Obviously, the two men were moving at a slow clip. The fence figured this lad was so far gone, he was not thinking too straight. Until the fence saw that totally lost look, he planned to bow out of the transaction. The fence could arrange a meeting to help Jess without the police. He planned on it.

"Derek, you're messed up."

"Why do you think that way?"

"I've been there. I know love when I see it."

He felt empathy for the man. Dean knew how strong Jess was as a person.

Dean said, "Jess is this spectacularly smart person in every class, totally blowing this old man's mind on his knowledge of safes out of the water, and dragged me into her higher world. I knew her way of thinking was way ahead of the normal brain. Jess is very special."

The old man saw that Derek believed Jess was special. It would take someone stronger to hold Jess. He wondered if this person could measure up to the task. The fence decided to help Derek.

"Jess is like my daughter and nothing happened on that date, so you can chill out. My daughter used to say this one word, *magical*. Jess said that word when we first met, and I was all the way in to helping her."

Derek did his research and knew that the fence's daughter died of an overdose of drugs, while the fence man was in prison for a year.

Derek acknowledged, "This whole set up was totally about Jess and her freedom."

The old man knew everything could work with his knowledge of the underworld. Both men relaxed and combined their superior minds. Derek and the fence agreed to set up the plan to catch the con artist killer. Derek arrived back at the docks in plenty of time to drive away with Jim.

The police were clueless until Derek chose to share the plan. He needed to talk with Jim about the proposed plan to catch the criminals and find out what he knew about Dean Crain.

17   Jess's Release

IT WAS NOON, and the jail clerk brought Jess her tray of food. The jail clerk knew it was enchilada day. The prisoner's lawyer was standing behind the jail clerk. The clerk unlocked the cell door and placed the food tray on the small bed. Her lawyer's name was Harv Macon from San Francisco. The front desk cleared him for entrance to his client's jail cell.

Harv handled her father's final house sale and estate closure. Dean gave her Harv's business card. That was how the two of them originally met. They dated for a while, and then Jess moved on telling him the distance between San Francisco and Los Angeles was too great.

Harv told her he could move. She didn't want him to lose his wealthy clients. Harv liked his rich friends.

Jess said, "Hello, Harv, it's been a while. How are you today?"

Harv laughed, "Same old Jess--friendly and cordial even in a jail cell. You look amazing for a jailbird, better than the last time I saw you. You look wonderfully happy, too."

Jess hugged him like an old friend and gave him a quick kiss. Harv held onto Jess a little bit longer than was required.

Harv said, "Can we make that kiss longer? I feel like we dropped something important. I miss our dates together. We make a good pair and my friends like you. I genuinely like you."

Jess pushed away from her friend and shook her head with a no signal. She told him about her investigator friend. In

65

other words, she was seeing someone. Harv was glad for her and unhappy for himself. The two of them sat down.

"I formulated your release paper. The request was dropping all charges against you and removal of the arrest record which could damage your reputation. The release was signed by my friend, Judge Spencer."

Harv and the Judge owned fishing boats and frequented the same favorite fishing holes and drank beer together after a good day. Jess knew the Judge and met him on occasion at Harv's modern hillside home. Harv made a point of locking into friends in high places for his future use. Jess sighed. It was the same person she dropped dating and here she was using him. At least, she was paying the bill. She would have to insist on it.

Harv went on to explain the reason for the release. "The police cannot hold you because there was insufficient evidence. However, they recommended you stay within two hundred miles of Napa for a few days. It's just a recommendation, not any kind of order."

"You brought blueprints, but also had blueprints of the other buildings on that side of the block because there used to be an old winery at that location and you were writing a book on the history of grapes. You were jogging and placed your heavy items under leaves so someone wouldn't steal them. You hurt from a muscle spasm and couldn't carry them anymore. The ropes were to do some climbing around the area."

"The jeweler's tools were always with you because you're a diamond expert who works in a jewelry store in Los Angeles. If you wanted to steal diamonds, you probably would have done so in Los Angeles, but you've been in the diamond industry for almost fifteen years, and there never existed any problems. Then there was written verification by the hotel clerk who was with you in your room fixing the TV at the time of the robbery and murder. The hotel clerk remembered talking with you about knitting and afghan blankets, so the judge signed the release. As soon as they complete their freaking forms, you could get your things and leave."

Then he continued, "I'm available for lunch. Would you like to come? There's a great restaurant that makes the plum-pork dough thing you like. I will cancel my important clients for you. I would love to talk with you. Did you know I bought one of your lighthouse photos? The photo matched the one you gave me for my office. You look hungry. Besides, the jail food didn't smell that interesting." Harv wasn't worried about her feelings for her new investigator friend. There was a chance that relationship would fail. If so, he would be there to pick up the pieces. He came a little closer and held her hand.

"Thanks, the restaurant sounded great, but I promised an old friend. Let's do lunch some other time." Jess gave him another hug and thanked him.

Harv was irritated. Jess was probably having lunch with his rich client, Dean Crain. Jess always turned to Dean. He pointed out that fact to her several times. Harv was unhappy about it, and she told him that her friends were her business.

Harv said, "Tell Dean hello. Oh, and tell him that I work during normal business hours."

Jess and her lawyer left the cell when the waiting jail clerk opened the door. The food tray was forgotten on the small bed. The next cell held two prostitutes, who finally were awake, and they immediately started fighting.

The jail clerk separated the two girls and put one of the prostitutes in Jess's old cell.

Jess retrieved her things and drove to Oakland to visit Dean Crain.

18   Dean's Sailboat

JESS ARRIVED AS Dean was sitting down to a large seafood salad and wine. Dean said, "Jess, glad to see you. I see sharp Harv got you released. Do you want some salad and wine?"

"Yes, please, I'm starving and haven't eaten." She grabbed some of the warm cheese balls and helped herself to the buffet. The small dessert crepes were for later. She missed Dean's chef-designed meals.

"Harv wanted to remind you to call him only during normal business hours."

Dean laughed, "Let me mention right back that Harv better watch his sorry behind. Harv Macon was lucky that good old Dean covered it many times." Then she asked, "How did everything go with Derek when he visited? My salad is scrumptious."

Dean leaned toward her and looked deeply at Jess.

"Okay, I really like the guy. I dated him a couple times before. He's nice and hot. We were together in Napa, and he invited me to a fancy restaurant for dinner. You remember how that worked." Jess smiled.

Dean looked pensive. He did, indeed, remember how that worked. He filled her in on the tentative plan.

"You could shed some light on that diamond necklace you wanted to buy in the underground. Perhaps you could fool the cops with your story about blueprints and tools. I know the use of some of your tools in the con artist world. I checked the coincidence of the Napa Jewelry store's safe. It matched their Safe manufacturing class. If you remember right, I was in jail once. I lived on the other side of the law earlier in my career.

What's up Jess? No secrets this time. No hiding things. I know you did that. Females did that, hide things from people they love. I will love you, no matter the problem."

"I know you love me. I love you immensely, but this is hard."

"I don't care how hard. Nothing is hard. It's a relative thing, sliding scale thing."

Jess knew he was trying to make her see that major things were minor.

"It hurts. I can't describe how I feel."

"I know you're hurting, but you need to stare the hurt in its sad face. I know you and whatever it is that you tried, it doesn't matter. You haven't obviously given up in the face of huge obstacles to get the necklace."

She had tried. Jess couldn't hide things from Dean anymore. "If I tell you the rest of the story, you must then promise to me that you know nothing about our conversation regarding the necklace."

He promised because Jess asked. She could always ask. No matter how small. He would listen. Dean learned to be a good listener.

"I went to Napa to steal a diamond necklace that belonged to my mother. Someone beat me to the job and killed people in the process. I saw the necklace before and held it in my hands when a crazy elderly lady came into the small jewelry shop where I had previously worked in Los Angeles. The crazy lady disappeared, and I could not find her again. When I was in Napa, I saw my mother's necklace. The Napa jeweler obviously switched the necklace on the old lady for a paste copy when she had her adopted son take the necklace there. The copy necklace was missing a ridge in the metal on the top of the clasp."

Jess drew a picture of the necklace and told Dean the size, quality, and number of stones and the dimensions of the clasp. She drew in the ridge for him. He touched the ridge on the drawing with his fingers.

"The crazy elderly woman was poisoned. Her paste copy necklace was missing just like the original necklace. Derek had explained to me why he was involved in the Napa case."

Dean asked, "Do you think the same person obtained both necklaces? Or do we have two different murderers, one a shooter and one the poisoner?"

"I remember the encounter the night of the robbery. Something about this whole thing was confusing. I feel there are complex people involved. Really scary people."

She went on to explain to him further that her father talked to Jess before he died from brain cancer. He told her that his first wife, her mom, died in a car accident which she already knew. Her real mom owned this beautiful diamond necklace given to her by royalty.

Dean got up, "Hold that thought, we're going to need more wine. Or at least, I'm going to need it. Or should I just get the scotch bottle?" Dean came through the galley door holding both bottles.

Jess continued with the conversation, telling him that her father had drawn a picture for her of the clasp and ridge.

"Your father remembered the necklace."

Jess said, "Yes, he did. When my mom died, the necklace disappeared from my parent's home. It was probably taken right after her funeral."

Dean said, "Stolen."

"Yes, someone stole it from their home. My father was upset because he wanted me to have the necklace. It was special from a trip the two of them had taken in Italy. My mom was a champion swimmer and won some medals. My father talked about a little child who almost drowned whom my mother saved. The family gave her the diamond necklace as a gift. The crazy lady told me the same story, only she substituted her name instead of my mother's. So, the old crazy woman was the thief and someone who knew my mother. She met her end via poison from some other evil con artist."

Dean was sitting in the upper deck chair shaking his head. "Why didn't you go to the police?"

"There was no documentation or proof and I found out about everything shortly before my father died."

"Didn't your father contact the police?"

"He did, but nothing ever came out of the investigation. I'm not sure if the report could still be found as the courthouse had a fire."

"What about the royal family that gave your mother the necklace?"

Jess was shown where the release was on the clasp. She told Dean she didn't have time to read the smaller name inside the clasp because the crazy woman yanked it out of her hands. Her father couldn't remember the name of the family from Italy.

Dean said, "There was an inside to the clasp?"

Jess said, "Yes, it was a special release lock, very hard to find."

"And she knew how to release the clasp. Unbelievable."

Jess and Dean sat back and relaxed.

Jess liked Dean's sailboat. He told her he quit fencing goods about ten years ago, but still knew his old cronies. Dean was very good at playing poker and won a lot of money. He won enough to be able to purchase the dream boat and condo in San Francisco. He still went gambling on occasion, but was mostly semiretired.

"I know your friend, Derek, already checked me out. That's okay with me as there isn't too much information out there. My old cronies are loyal because I give them loans on occasion. They always pay me back."

Dean knew how all the fence games worked.

19   Food Tray at the Jail Cell

DEREK INTERRUPTED DEAN and Jess's day. Derek rubbed his hands through his hair three times now. He went to the jail and to her cell. There was some other woman in there. They were zipping the bag and removing the body from the jail cell. "Why hadn't Jess let me know her lawyer got her released?"

He saw that she had called, but didn't leave a message.

The jail clerk explained to Derek when the food tray was delivered, and that Jess and her lawyer were together the whole time until he let them out. The jail clerk forgot about the food tray in her cell. He didn't think she ate anything though, because her lawyer asked her to lunch. The lawyer person kissed the woman, told her she looked amazing, held her hand, and hugged her real close. They talked for a long time.

One look at Derek's face and the jail clerk immediately shut up. Derek looked surprised and agitated. The jail clerk didn't tell him the lady told the poor guy no to the lunch date.

Derek called Jess and didn't wait for her to speak when she picked up. "Where are your coordinates? Are you with someone right now?"

"Hello, honey, my tails should know my location."

Derek halted a minute, "Jess, this situation is like your something Tomales Bay situation."

Jess received the quick message and said, "I'm with Dean Crain on his sailboat docked at Oakland."

He was immensely relieved, "Did you eat any of the jail food?"

"No, I ate lunch with Dean."

"Jess, honey, put Dean on the phone."

Jess gave Dean the phone. Jess saw Dean's eyes turn dark. "We'll take the boat out in the Bay until we hear from you. I'll have the crew move the boat immediately."

Dean handed Jess the phone and called out orders to his crew to untie the boat, start engine, and haul themselves out of there now. His crew knew what *now* meant. It meant faster than normal, supersonic speed.

Dean had explained to them his command meaning of *now*. Whatever the owner of the boat wanted, the crew never hesitated. Dean paid them well and took care of them.

Dean told Jess, "Below deck now."

Jess quickly moved, also knowing the command, and talked with Derek.

"Do whatever Dean asked you to do and be safe."

"Is it bad?"

"Yes, the food tray, probably poison. It was a young prostitute. The food tray was in the cell that you left earlier."

Jess understood and hung up, sitting down in the plush lower deck inside lounge. She remembered the food tray on the jail bed. Jess came to the upper deck when Dean gave her the "all clear" message. The boat boys decided to head out of the bay for a couple of hours. Jess and everyone on board rode a great ride as the swells of the ocean were just right for their size boat.

Dean purchased the boat heavily loaded with gear, which made sailing that much easier. He bought every bell and whistle and kept the boat maintained by a team of experts. He talked a little about buying a larger motorboat. He wanted to have a helicopter on board. Dean already looked at some of the new toys and wished he hadn't. All he dreamt about now was that new motorboat. His crew would stay with him, of course.

The boat eventually headed back toward the Bay because the sun was setting.

XXXXXX

Derek was still at the jail with the hysterical prostitute who stayed in her cell. She would only drink sealed bottles of juice. Simms was getting statements from everyone at the jail. Rutherford was outside trying to keep the crowd away from the coroner's vehicle.

The scene was utter chaos which was what the killer wanted, but he couldn't see the victim as the body was zippered up. The police were all quiet and wouldn't talk to the outsiders.

Jim Michaels was back at the hotel making phone calls to find a safe place for Jess.

Derek was wracking his brain trying to figure out why the killer wanted to hurt Jess. What did Jess know that made her a target? There must be something she hadn't told him.

The other possibility scared him even more. Somehow the psychopathic poisoner was obsessed with her. If so, she was in very real danger due to the creep's mentally warped mind. That concept was mind-boggling. Putting poison in a prisoner's meal meant this person had no fear of the police and was quite able to slip in and out easily. He knew obsession started slow and grew into an unstoppable force. The killing force would continue until they could bring the villain permanently down. He was worried.

20   Safe House

NOW THAT JESS was safely out of jail, Derek and Dean could work together with more relaxed minds on the fence set up to catch the killer. First order of business was to guard and deliver Jess to a safe place. Derek was going to miss sleeping with her every night. Jess called her work place, and they were okay with the extra couple weeks off.

Jess went to the safe house in San Francisco. It was in a nicely furnished condo down the block from Dean's place. The condo was on the third floor and contained a very private back garden balcony, and even a small tree. There was a gas barbeque grill outside and a small store with bread, milk, eggs, sandwiches, beer, etc. on the first floor. The parking area was an underground garage with stairs or elevator.

Dean, Derek, Jim, and Jess were in her condo. Jim got along very well with Dean because they were about the same age and had lots of stories to tell. The boys thought they were going to leave Jess out of the fence planning.

Jess told them, "No way. I want to be in the planning."

The police brought Detective Dave Paulson to Napa to handle the prostitute murder case so Derek could use his time on the project. That's what they decided to call everything--the project. Jim picked up groceries.

Dean hired one of his lady friends to pick up some comfortable clothes, shoes, and makeup for Jess. The lady brought the clothes to the boat when they came into the harbor and moored the boat.

Jess put the salad on the table. She set the table and opened the merlot wine bottle. Dean and Jim grilled the steaks.

She checked the garlic bread in the broiler. They ate the delicious grilled dinner. Afterwards there was ice cream for dessert and bananas. Jim picked up bananas for Jess. He apologized, because they didn't have banana ice cream. It was her favorite. Jess made a last batch of coffee.

Derek finally took an opportunity to talk with Jess in private. Derek asked, "Will you please leave me a message when you call so that I would know that you're all right? Your lawyer, Harv, got you released. When I saw the body in the cell, I thought it was you. It could have been you. Sometimes you drive me crazy with worry. I know I'm stressing out. I'm having a hard time concentrating and trying to protect you at the same time. The jail scene was nuts with the dead body and the other prostitute."

Jess shook her head up and down. She wondered if he knew about her relationship with Harv. This was probably not a good time to talk about old boyfriends. "Yes, I will leave a message always."

Derek asked, "What else do you know about the diamond necklace? I think you're in danger from the creep poisoner. I need facts."

Jess reluctantly repeated what she told Dean that day. She asked that he not divulge the information to anyone about the internal clasp inscriptions that she had partially seen. Because they would also know the inscription was "To Sami." She called her mother that when she was little because it was hard to say the word, Samantha.

Derek sat there in stunned silence.

Jess got up from the soft comfortable leather couch and went outside to her patio with the two old guys. She spoke too soon. Derek wasn't ready to hear her truths. She felt that way when she was in jail. What she planned was too much for him to understand. This was now a large point of contention between them. It was about trust. Derek was big on her being real with him.

76

She planned to rob a bank. Who takes a Safe class to rob a bank for a family heirloom? That was more nuts. How could he trust her? He didn't know if he should be sad or glad about the information she disclosed. He was now more confused. All the nights together, why hadn't she trusted him?

Derek decided he was going to stay the night. He needed to hold onto Jess after the fiasco at the jail cell. His feelings were stuck and turbulence about Jess was churning in his mind. Everyone ate their steaks and Dean and Jim quickly exited the scene to get away from two confused and very quiet friends. They made plans to meet again the next morning.

21   The Real Fences

DEAN AND DEREK were in their element planning the project. A price of two hundred thousand dollars was agreed for the diamond necklace because of the interesting, unprovable royalty concept that had been thrown on the table.

The newbie fences were happy with the amount. The stage was warehouse number 41 in the garment district on a Saturday evening at midnight when the yards and warehouses were empty in San Francisco.

The night watchman was paid on the side to disappear from the location for three hours during the night with assurances it was just an outside transaction. All the watchmen knew what outside meant. It meant illegal.

Derek ran a check on the night watchman, who was divorced and paying heavy monthly alimony to the ex-wife. He was friends with a new chickie that liked to use his charge cards, too.

The fence money was obtained from the police department and placed in a duffel bag of small denomination bills. Dean would be the delivery boy with a speaker in his ear and microphone implanted in the bill of his hat. He just needed to stay out in the open. No problem.

Dean hired some of his old cronies and told them to bring artillery. He didn't quite tell Derek about the artillery, but figured Derek was a smart boy and would understand the logic. He also hired a fireworks guy, if needed, just to scare the hell out of the newbies. The signal was a lift of his ball cap. He did tell Derek about that fact. Both Derek's and Jim's eyes lit up with laughter. Everyone was ready, and Jess was safe at her condo with Jim.

Dean's vehicle was this heavy, huge-tired, high-speed engine, dark gray truck. The rest of the crew drove generic vehicles that looked like they belonged at a warehouse. Now the boys forgot to check the weather as a storm front was moving in.

The newbies arrived, and the cronies were hidden with the fireworks guy. The only police were Derek and a few other guys. Dean pulled up in his truck and jumped out with the duffel bag scaring a few of the newbies a few feet back.

Dean knew a person always must remain confident like a lion or bear or something vicious. He did make growling sounds on occasion. That made the newbies really scared because then they thought he was crazy.

"The newbies want the money right away from the other fence."

Dean smiled and said softly, "More stupid dimwits."

The cronies almost gave away their location trying to hold in their laughter.

Dean motioned to the leader. The leader was always the guy heavily tattooed with fake diamond earrings and a red shirt. The leader didn't seem to get that the red glows in the dark and made him a perfect target every time.

The electronic tail was implanted on the newbies' cars by the silent police detail.

Dean talked slowly to the leader explaining, "You must show the goods as that was the only way my rich client did these wonderful transactions. If your boys wanted future business from my very rich client, then you must follow those rules, or very, very rich client will walk away from the deal. Do you understand, or should I repeat it slower?"

The leader wasn't sure if the fence guy was pulling his leg or not.

Dean, tired of waiting for the leader to figure out the mystery of this transaction, growled.

The leader received the impatient message and knew he was inexperienced, he motioned to his second boy to bring the necklace.

Dean was handed the necklace, and he checked it out, holding it up and twirling it under the dim streetlight. He ran his hand over the clasp. He stopped and said quietly, "No ridge."

Derek swore, "Geez, it's the fake necklace. Stupid con artists." The he said into the microphone, "Take it and pass the money. Exit and tails were on the villain."

Dean put the paste necklace in his zipper pocket and zipped it shut while handing the duffel bag to the leader. The newbie boys looked quickly in the bag seeing the green money and backed away.

Dean moved to the truck, put keys in the ignition, and leaned out to shut the door. Meanwhile, Derek and cops were moving out as were the cronies. A gust of wind lifted Dean's baseball cap totally off. The cops and cronies saw it and started running to their vehicles. Dean retrieved his hat quickly.

The firework's guy was a little shaky because Dean told him no liquor on the job. He finally lighted his three-second-delay package and headed toward his truck. The newbies were still walking backward when Dean spun out of the parking lot.

The noise and fireworks combined into total lighted sky to scare the living crap out of the newbies as they ran, stumbling into each other. Dean was laughing and thinking those were the good old days. He sometimes missed that type of business.

Derek and his team of cops were tracking the electronic tail.

The old cronies just wanted to do that again real soon. This show had been a pleasurable one. Nobody got hurt today.

22   Arrest of Murderers

JIM CALLED DEREK on his cell.

Jim said, "We have a small-town female cop at a cemetery close by, the Napa tail. Do you want me to head there? Dean's people are here."

"Thanks for continuing the monitor on the tail. Hurry to the cemetery and do it quietly. I'm not sure what the tail would be doing here. We've kept this stakeout quiet." Derek knew that Jess was safe with Dean's cronies. He was glad she became sensible about staying out of this scene. It had been hard to convince her that the police also didn't want to have to watch after her. Dean convinced her.

Jim responded, "Like the freaking dead."

Derek called in the backup team and briefed them on the net closure. Other teams followed the stragglers that were moving in the opposite direction and would arrest them.

"The leader with the duffel bag was, get this, driving a red car. His license plate showed the letters G-L-O and then zero-zero-zero-zero."

Wait until Derek told Dean that little scenario. It was the number of zeroes. Wasn't there a children's game called "Out". Four times you are "It" and then you are out of the game. This group of criminals were not your average group of bullies. Their intelligence was in question. Dean turned the necklace over to one of Derek's backup team members and headed on home to return the vehicle and exchange off the license plate the police provided.

The police waited silently for the newbies to hand the money to the perp. The place was a large park on the other side of the cemetery. The newbies made the exchange and the local cops waited. Derek saw that the person who was the receiver of the duffel bag was another different tribe newbie. There were layers of con artists involved.

Derek said into his radio, "Hold until you see where this person moved. Let the perp lead you further so you catch all of them."

Everyone waited for different tribe guy to start moving. This guy got into a white car. Derek now laughed. It showed very shiny rims on the tires. Derek thought, *this bust was a walk in the park.* Only he said it into the radio, giving all the police a fun night to remember.

Jim let Derek know on his cell, "A white car entered the cemetery."

Derek asked, "Super shiny rims in cemetery?" with his radio left open. "Why do they always pick the cemetery? I guess it's because everyone is dead, even the ghosts. Or maybe it's because there are no cops in a cemetery. Won't they be surprised?"

"Roger that."

The small Napa town cop car moved toward the white car. Both people got out of their vehicles. Derek talked into the radio, "It's not Detective Sally Rutherford, not sure who this person is in the police vehicle. Check the system to see if Ms. Rutherford from Napa reported her vehicle as stolen."

The duffel bag was passed. Derek told his team, "Move in."

Derek and the cops caught the perp and a young woman possibly related to Rutherford. The different tribe newbie was surprised that he was arrested. They were read their rights and taken to jail. The young woman was Rutherford's wild, younger sister, who was in love with different tribe newbie.

They figured he was the man who dreamed up the plot with the jeweler's wife to get money and then shot three people.

His thirty-eight pistol was in the white car and jammed in the glove compartment.

Derek told the police to check the man's DNA for comparison on the jeweler's wife murder. He calculated the man possibly was her lover boyfriend. If he was, then the Rutherford younger sister would spill every piece of information regarding the man.

Detective Sally Rutherford was called in to talk with her sister and get legal counsel. Rutherford didn't look happy. She had been tailing the wrong person, and she did not secure her police vehicle. Her superiors would have a lot of questions regarding those facts.

Derek went to Jess's condo and let Dean and Jim know the outcome of the whole mess.

Jess welcomed Derek into the bedroom with open arms. "You're my hero. The murderer was caught with his accomplice."

Derek worried that the whole business wasn't over yet. He knew they only scratched the surface. The real diamond necklace was missing, as was the poisoner. He felt major feelings of doom headed their way. Dean looked out of his condo window and felt the same edginess.

Later, Jess worried about the complex person in the ring.

Jim had no clue the monster psycho was someone he was going to run into shortly.

23   Real Con Artist and Psycho

JIM RECEIVED A call from the schoolteacher friend. She needed his help. Jim could come to her room when he arrived at the hotel. Jim knocked on the hotel room, and the door opened.

The next thing he knew he was going down after a slight prick on his neck. He awoke in a cave-like room, fully gagged and tied up. So was the schoolteacher friend. She was still out cold from the drugs.

It was damp and cold in the room. The walls were rock-hard. It was so dark, he couldn't tell what type of rock. He knew the soil around Napa was mostly clay-loam soil for the Shiraz vineyards and mainly sandy-loam in Sonoma. The loamy soil helped produce high quality grapes for wine. He really hadn't heard anyone mention any caves in the area. He wondered if this was at one time an old vineyard cave used for storing wine in oak barrels. If so, there were no barrels or equipment around. Jim shivered, and he was glad he still wore his jacket. Looking at the schoolteacher, she had a sweater on over her jeans and hiking shoes. *Her shoe laces might come in handy*, thought Jim. He examined the room for any other objects or escape routes.

There was only a heavy wooden door. The door suddenly swung open and Jim was surprised to see the person that appeared. Jim felt conned.

There was a table and chair to the left with syringes and bottles of solutions, which were either drugs or poison. On the table were Jim's cell phone, keys, key fob, hat, sunglasses, wallet, coin purse, and hanky. His revolver was in the backpack in the front seat of the rental car back at the hotel and rifle with scope in the trunk. His gun still had the night scope on.

"Bad luck."

He saw water running down a wall and disappearing under the floor, probably some rainwater or spring. The con artist psycho approached the girl and gave her another syringe of liquid.

"Well," Jim figured, "she was going to be out for a while."

Then the con artist psycho approached Jim and took his gag off. Psycho told Jim, "You can yell all you want because no one will hear you."

Jim asked the question, "Why have you kidnapped us? What purpose is there in this venture? Neither one of us is rich enough for a ransom." Anyway, Jim hoped his newly-found friend wasn't rich. He didn't know too much about her yet. Jim didn't care about himself that much. Not too many people would miss him. Still, he wasn't ready to die without a fight.

The psycho replied, "Why not?"

Jim knew this was not going to be a good time. He wished he was back in the cemetery--a safer place--or around the newbie fences, where there were just children playacting.

Now the nutcase in front of him was very real. He must find out what he wanted from Jim. He knew the schoolteacher friend was only the bait. Jim was going to find out soon enough what was his fate.

The psycho said two words, "Jess Jameson."

Jim spoke, "Piece of crap."

The psycho jumped up and down screaming.

Jim thought to himself that this guy had buttons he could push to his advantage.

The psycho came over totally calmed down, studying Jim as if he were some lab rat specimen. Psycho spoke, "Where is she?"

Jim played dumb, "She's over there in the chair and you're a psychobabble piece of crap." Same thing happened-- more jumping up and down and screaming.

Now there were some young people walking the woods and they heard this odd screaming noise. They heard it twice now and quickly picked up their blanket and beer heading back home in their car. Their favorite meeting place destroyed forever. They informed their other friends who would finally inform the cops of the location.

Psycho picked up a different syringe and walked over to schoolteacher. He told Jim, "This one will cause her heart to stammer and stutter violently. There would be blinding pain, and then she would die. You must know I killed at least three people?"

Jim wondered who the third person could possibly be that the madman murdered. He knew about the elderly woman in Los Angeles and the female prostitute at the jail in Napa. This was information the police needed to know. The psycho made a slip. Jim tried to get more information.

"Who's the third person? Was it your last date?"

The psycho hit him on the side of the head. Jim winced. He shouldn't have asked about the madman's dating habits. It looked to be a sore spot. Madman probably wasn't that much fun anyway. His finesse in the dating game was in question as well as personality. A trickle of blood rolled down his check from the cut. The creep wore a gold ring which had scraped his cheek. He wondered if the ring was stolen. He thought this was more than likely.

Jim told him he did not need to hurt the schoolteacher because she had not done anything wrong. She was a nice lady and probably didn't remember a thing about tonight. She isn't a party to any of this business. The psycho stopped and thought. "Then you will tell me where Jess is located?"

"Sure, lots of people know Jess is on Dean Crain's sailboat, although sometimes she went shopping, but then most women do. Mine sure did, especially the makeup counter on sale day. Horrified me to think of all that money gone to waste when I could have bought fish bait. You know, buy the good stuff and jazzy fish lures. Maybe a new rod and reel would be better than that fourth tube of lipstick she bought. I also have a hole in my net, so a nice new one would have helped the last time that I went deep sea fishing with my friend. Now, my friend has a nice fishing tub. I sort of wish that I was on the tub today instead of in this cave. Maybe you can let us go. You could consider that effort a good-will gesture. It would be a gift out of the kindness of your heart, but then what was I thinking? Anyone who kidnaps people probably doesn't have one or else it's on the wrong side of your body which might explain a lot."

Psycho interrupted his speech. "Shut up. I don't care about your fishing habits. You're wasting my time. Where is this sailboat?"

Jim hesitated and then remembered what day it was. He gave psycho the Harbor name and boat slip number.

Psycho gave Jim a shot of the smaller syringe, so he could take off for Oakland. He couldn't miss finding her. Jim knew he was safe for now, and he bought himself some time. He hoped it would be enough for Simms or Derek to find them. Psycho left the cave with the key left in the lock on the outside. In a rush to make his plan and get everything ready, he missed taking the key.

Now Jim talked with Dean about boats when they first met. Jim wanted to buy himself a fishing tub. He had been saving his money for a long time. Currently, he hired a boat to take him fishing. Jim knew the sailboat was in a slip far away from everyone else's boat because Dean could afford privacy. No one was ever on the boat Sunday or Monday because his boys went into San Francisco to party.

Jim just hoped they caught that stupid sack of psycho-poison babble in time. He already was thinking about the key as he started to fall deeper into unconsciousness. He was glad he worked out at the gym, as the drug didn't have the same effect on his body as the schoolteacher. He wished he had his rifle. Life was so simple when a person had the advantage. He wasn't going to give this creep any more advantage.

Perhaps he could think real hard and send a message to Dean. He wished he knew how to do telepathy. Maybe he should have taken a class or at least dated that gypsy girl long ago. Now, she was pretty and mysterious. He remembered her silky, dark long hair. Her hands were always warm. She was good people. He was not ready for her kind. She told Jim that if he ever needed her, he was to send her a message. He didn't get how she could hear any message. She assured him that she could hear it. Jim hadn't quite trusted her words, but now, he needed help.

It might be a good time to give his gypsy friend a mental message. What could it hurt? He had to believe in something. Heaven was approaching too close to him in the cave. The cave was emitting creaks and sounds. There was a knocking somewhere. It could be a rat scurrying in and out the door. He wondered if he was losing his mind. He thought Heaven could wait a little longer. His body wasn't ready. It occurred to him that now would be a good time to send a prayer, just to be on the safe side. He hadn't prayed since his wife died. He sent the prayer. His wife would have explained to him that it was a wise thing to do.

Panic then hit Jim. He couldn't remember her name, the gypsy woman. "Was it Maria; no, it was Marla. But Marla what?" Desperation was rolling past his brain as he reached into long term memory and visualized her image. "It's Marla de Marco." Relief surrounded him. Jim sent his silent message to her, the gypsy woman, praying again that it would be received. Maybe she was some earthen angel. He hoped so. He needed armies of angels on his side or an encampment of circular wagons loaded with gypsies, preferably with their hand guns filled with bullets. He'd take archery arrows with fire or anything else in a gypsy arsenal or even a fishing net would do. He could whack the bad guy over the head with it and tie him up with the netting real tight. It was too bad there weren't a few alligators in the wetlands where Jim could drop him off. Or better yet, put him on the fishing boat and drop psycho near the Farallon Islands.

"Send everything!" The message went over the air waves.

Then Jim's head slumped. His burst of frenetic energy was gone; he was out.

24   Sailboat Here Gone

PSYCHO COLLECTED EVERYTHING ready in the trunk of his car by noon Sunday. He drove to Oakland to wait until dark. Psycho was suddenly hungry. He forgot to eat the day before in his excitement. There was a hamburger joint a mile away from the boat docks.

He disappeared to get a hamburger, fries, and soda. There was a light on inside the boat and the curtains were drawn when he arrived back to the boat dock. Psycho thought, "Good, she was on board."

He snuck on top of the boat around midnight, planting his devices in strategic spots around the outside of the boat. The security system recorded his movements and sent the data to Dean's computer.

Derek left messages all day for Jim and received no response. He called the hotel. They saw both enter the hotel separately, but didn't see them leave. There was an empty food cart outside the room which later appeared by an exit door that was partially open. He called the schoolteacher's room, but there was no response.

Derek called Simms and asked him to check the hotel or around town. He knew something was up because Jim loved his phone and always carried it on him. Two people didn't vanish in thin air, except they had.

Simms found Jim's car in the lot and checked the trunk. "Nice rifle."

He picked the long rifle up and checked the scope. "Powerful piece of equipment." Simms bet Jim wished he was holding the gun right now, especially if he was in danger.

Then he checked their hotel rooms. No schoolteacher and no Jim. He found an empty syringe in the garbage in the schoolteacher's room. She didn't appear the druggy type at all. Simms bagged the syringe and quickly called back Derek and relayed the information. "He was thinking along the lines of a kidnaper poisoner."

Derek said, "Put a trace out now on them. Talk to everyone, even the teenagers. They are in trouble." He worked with Jim in the past. The kidnaper took Jim because he possibly knew where Jess was located. Jim would try to protect the schoolteacher and Jess. If Jim had to disclose Jess, he would point to some other location. That was the way Jim worked. But where would he send the kidnaper? He knew Jim would use the ruse to give them time to find them. They didn't have much time to find Jim and his friend.

Derek called Dean to go watch Jess as trouble was coming. He gave Dean a brief synopsis of the psycho kidnaper and poisoner. Dean understood and called his San Francisco cronies for extra hidden guards on Jess. He told them to bring the artillery. Dean would rain hellfire on that guy if he tried to touch Jess. He hoped Jim could hold on until they found him.

Jim awoke again, and it was dark in the cave. He jumped his chair closer. Jim's body hit on the door, and the movement knocked the key out of the lock. Then he maneuvered his body up the chair until his shoes were close to his hands. He touched the inner sole of his shoe and out popped the long knife. He got the tape cut off his hands and feet and removed the tape from the schoolteacher. He took the used tapes and made a wand out of it to put under the door to slide the key toward him.

Jim smiled, "Psycho can't get in unless he brought a second key which he doubted. The guy wasn't that smart."

Jim went to the table and picked up his cell phone which lit up with "no service." He hit the special flashlight app button and quickly put one of the little syringes in his pocket filled with liquid just in case, emptied the rest of the junkie stuff in a low corner of the cave and moved the table directly over the liquid.

Taking his wallet, he put everything in his pocket and used the wallet like a cup to get some water off the wall. He took the schoolteacher's laces out and made a noose out of them. Then he picked up his key fob which contained a heavy dose Vitamin C, and took one. Inside the fob were a metal wire and a small tool. He started working on the screws on the old-fashioned door.

It was exactly one in the morning when Dean couldn't sleep. Something Derek said nagged at his brain. Jim would send the killer to a location different from where Jess was.

The sailboat was a different location. He remembered talking with Jim about his boat schedule, special lighting, automatic curtain closers, and hidden cameras. The hidden cameras were the key. "Hello, Jim, I received your message. Check the boat cameras."

He turned on the notebook computer, which he brought over to Jess's house and retrieved the latest instant camera videos that captured all movement. He watched the sneaky psycho move around his sailboat. It looked like he was planting packages on the boat.

Dean called up Jorge who always stayed in Oakland and didn't go with the boys to San Francisco. He told Jorge, "Check out the sailboat now with armor."

Dean called Derek and let him know what he saw on his computer. It was exactly 1:10 when the seventy-five-foot sailboat blew in the biggest bonfire ever seen in this harbor. It was a total, huge insurance loss. Dean ordered all kinds of insurance on that sailboat.

Jorge had a camera on his cell phone. He grabbed his gun and headed over to the harbor. He was there before the fire department and police. Jorge took photos of the blown sailboat and sent them to Dean.

Dean did a dance in the living room. "Dream motorboat now coming my way with helicopter."

Then he called back Derek. Derek shook his head, "Psycho person just ramped up the investigation to involve at least one hundred to two hundred or more cops."

Psycho con artist person was driving back across the bridge to the cave to dispose of the bodies.

25   Finding Jim

IT WAS MIDNIGHT, and Simms went to the bar in another town to talk with their customers. Several of the patrons knew this young couple who heard some strange noises around Trenton Road.

Simms knew there were a lot of old caves in the area and headed back to town to get more help and the dogs. He also brought ropes, flashlights, blankets, water, and some candy bars. He had to awaken a lot of people, but they didn't mind. Jim was one of their own.

They arranged to meet at the edge of the next town outside the bar where the young couple had been. The fire truck even arrived in case they were needed.

The dogs were the answer to Jim and the schoolteacher's rescue. The rescuers kept calling and Jim heard them and started hollering like psycho boy. Jim wanted to see the daylight again.

The dogs' ears picked up the echo immediately and found the cave entrance. They were going to need the fire truck's hatchets when suddenly Jim slid the key under the door to Simms.

Simms scratched his head, "Well, he was shocked, there was a key."

The door opened. A groggy schoolteacher was led out by Jim. Blankets, water, and candy bars were given to them. Jim pulled Simms aside and gave him the description of psycho person. Simms couldn't believe it and put out a trace bulletin, "Proceed with caution, possible multiple murderer."

Jim used Simms phone to contact Derek with the information. He told him about the possibility of a third person the Psycho poisoned. Derek immediately distributed the information, called Dean, and headed towards Jess's condo. Jim showed Simms the cave and where the poison was poured out and the syringe wrapped in his white handkerchief that may possibly contain the psycho's possible fingerprints.

Simms was happy Jim was safe and would be able to shoot his wonderful rifle with the scope. That made Jim laugh. He admitted to Simms that for a while he wasn't sure he would see his rifle again. He felt the danger was a little too close. Jim was glad they brought in the dogs.

Jim asked Simms if he wanted to go fishing sometime in San Francisco as a thank-you. He could tell him a cool story about a gypsy woman. Simms liked fishing; gypsies also sounded interesting. He had a few good friends that liked to rub the crystal ball on occasion. He, personally, didn't believe in the stuff, which his friends forgave him. He would arrange the vacation anytime Jim could get away from his busy retired life. He also had quite a few new lures he hadn't tested yet. Jim could help with that. Jim smiled. He thought somehow his message to the gypsy lady was more than adequately heard. How did Simms know about his wish for lures?

Psycho person saw the fire truck and cop cars and exited the area immediately heading towards his stash and the diamond necklace in the leather pouch. He needed to move fast to make it out of town. He buried the box with the necklace inside. He ditched his leased car in the woods close to the bus stop and hid until morning. He already changed clothes and put on a new identity.

The police were investigating psycho's apartment and the jewelry store again to check the safe. All the jewels were taken to a special safe location except the stolen ones. But they needed to recheck. He could be hiding anywhere, anywhere a worm or lizard could go.

26   The Salamander

BILL BARKER WAS the con artist, the jewelry store clerk that helped Jess the first day with the small colored diamond necklaces when she arrived in Napa. He was the person who talked with Derek initially about the missing jewelry items.

Bill was the person who kidnapped and drugged Jim and the schoolteacher. He was the poisoner of two known victims and one unknown victim. He was the bomb expert who blew up a sailboat and destroyed a boat dock in the city of Oakland.

No one saw this guy coming. He was truly the psycho con artist. They had his hand writing sample, fingerprints, and DNA from his hotel room comb. The police obtained nothing else to catch this guy. He slipped through the cracks and was out in the world. The con artist was gone for now.

So, the police found out Bill Barker was an alias. The real Bill Barker's body washed up onshore one day. The unknown poison victim was found. The poison victim had been one of those kids who tried college for a few years and then dropped out due to their marijuana habit. The real Bill worked a summer job picking grapes in the wine country. It was a very unfortunate day when the young man ran into the killer on a bus.

Bill told the killer all his personal history, enough for the killer to create his next resume. The real Bill had just cashed his checks and was flush with money on his way back home.

The killer easily got the drop on the friendly guy when he invited him to his home and they walked the half mile to his parent's home. All identification cards and money were now in the killer's hands. The body was dumped near a little stream that grew to a raging river, which emptied into the ocean when the heavy rain came.

Jess, Derek, Dean, and Jim were at her condo. The group finished an early dinner of Chinese takeout. Jess ate Moo Shu pork, and the men chowed down Spicy Mandarin Chicken. The men were talking after dinner when Jess picked up her notebook and read her "Grapes History" notes.

Jess said, "He wore green contacts. His eyes were brown."

The men stop talking. Jess explained she saw the rims of the contacts when the light caught his eye as he turned his head to talk to another salesclerk. "He also had a small devil head tattoo about one half an inch under his watch on the left hand."

She picked up a pad and pencil and drew the image. Then she handed the drawing to Derek. "He wore a strange ring. It was like a classroom ring but different and all gold. It was similar in size to a small fish in a pond."

She drew a picture of the ring and all the men looked at it. Derek put that piece of paper with the other one.

"His belt was a hammered silver buckle with brown leather. He wore brown Italian shoes."

"How did she know they were Italian?" Dean raised his hand, because he wore Italian shoes and Jess commented on his shoes when he wore them.

Derek left to provide the information to his superiors. Derek was upset that Jess had been so close to psycho killer. The feelings of helplessness started weaving in his soul. How could he protect Jess? The danger level was very high. And why hadn't she trusted him? His world was falling apart. He needed to be better at his job.

Dean talked with Jess and Jim about the killer. "The killer reminded him of a word his cronies used. The word was *salamander,* which meant cold-blooded, slippery, and hidden until night when they became a voracious feeder. Their ability to camouflage their exterior helped them survive from a tadpole until it turned into the tailed lizard. In ancient times, people believed it was a mythical creature that breathed fire, much like the dragon, and they were the benders of fire in Hades. Some lizards escaped from Hades and grew lungs walking upon the land."

Jim got up from the couch. "The poison was part of their killer's controlled fascination of the hellfire."

Both Jess and Dean acknowledged with a nod of their heads. "The killer would be called the Greek word, s*alamander*." Dean believed Jess when she told him the killer was complex and scary. From now on, nothing would surprise Dean about the creepy poisoner.

He tangled with scary before. It was the sliding scale thing. Sometimes a person needed to rig the scale in their favor to help it balance. Dean was good at doing just that. A reptile was just a reptile. Dean put a note to himself to check how much it would cost to put guns on his helicopter.

27   Trouble between Lovers

JIM, DEAN, AND Jess waited for Derek to return. He did so, and they shared with him the Salamander story. Then Jess stood up and paced the room. "I know a way to catch the killer. He had tried to kill me, so his obsession could be his weakness."

She explained the project plot to them. "We will throw a large party on Dean's new boat with the helicopter offshore. The party would be a wedding. It's a wedding between me and Derek. I will be the bait. The killer will come because they will put my picture, our picture in the paper. The police can lay their own con artist trap for the killer. They have sharpshooters and could take the evil one out. That's something the killer hasn't planned on. The police will be hidden. They will outsmart the evil poisoner. It can work. It won't be a real wedding, just pretend."

Dean and Jim both said, "It might work."

Derek's face was red. He jumped off the couch, "Are you absolutely crazy to put yourself in that much danger? That evil guy will kill you. Your plan is nuts much like your robbery scheme. You have no idea how to rob a bank or catch a killer. A fake wedding. How does a person plan pretend? I don't have to pretend anything, because I won't be a party to such an absurd plan. I wonder why I'm even here."

Dean went, "Oh, no, wrong way."

Stomping off to the bedroom, Jess locked the door. Derek was mad that she shut the door. He left the condo with the bottle of whiskey and drove his car to the beach, staying there all night.

Jim and Dean decided they better stay overnight. Dean grabbed the couch, and Jim took the lounge chair that folded back.

Jess was in the bedroom and slowly moved off the bed. She started packing all her stuff in the backpack and lightweight duffle bag. She held her rental car keys and made all her decisions in her head, step-by-step. Taking her cell phone, she made the airplane reservations. She called her manager at the jewelry store and left him the message that she was quitting her job for personal reasons. Then she followed through with an e-mail to the manager and an e-mail to her apartment manager.

At three o'clock in the morning, she left the condo with a short note for Derek. The note contained a minimal amount of words as it said, "Good-bye. Don't tail me anymore."

She waited long enough. Jess tried their relationship. She couldn't do this. Their differences were major. Derek didn't need to protect her anymore. No one did. She handled things just fine before.

The two men were out of this hemisphere due to too much wine after the disaster show. She easily slipped by the San Francisco crony guards. She took the earliest flight out, turned in her rental car, and put her gear in the trunk of her vehicle. She went to her apartment and threw her clothes and shoes in the car. Leaving the dishes, silverware, pots, and pans and bedding for the next client was all right per the landlord. She left her apartment keys and a final check for an additional month's rent and cleaning fees.

She cut her front hair into bangs, put the dark blonde hair color in and the purple strands of dye. Washing the color solution off, she left her hair to wet dry.

Jess took the special hippie outfit out of the closet and found the cheap hoop earrings. All her gold and diamond jewelry were put in a velvet bag and then into the backpack.

She grabbed two plastic bins and her light-toned sunglasses and put them on. Getting in her car with the items, she stopped at the large dumpster for the Helping Hands

Charity. One by one, she dropped the clothes and shoe items in the narrow slot.

Then she stopped for gas, a sandwich, chips, and soda. She went to her bank and closed her account, withdrawing some cash, traveler's checks, and a certified check for the balance. Not stopping for any change of address at the post office, she also turned in her phone for a new one with a new number.

XXXXXX

Derek woke up around nine o'clock the next morning and saw several messages from Dean. He then looked out his window at the cop motioning him to roll down his window. Derek showed the cop his identification and stepped out of the car to walk to the coffee shop. He got his coffee and ate his egg sandwich as he drove back to Jess's condo. He was at the door, so he did not call Dean.

Derek walked in the condo and felt the weight of doom. Dean and Jim didn't look him in the eye. Dean handed him the note. The bedroom door was open, and Jess was not in the condo. Reading the note Derek sat down on the couch. "I've been really stupid. She ran again."

All he felt was pain. He knew the pain would not go away. Derek ran his hands through his hair. "Now what do we do?" Misery was going to haunt him. There was no opera song he could think of to describe the desperation knocking his brain.

Dean and Jim left Derek alone and exited the condo. Dean arrived home and decided to go down to his new motorboat moored in the harbor because the new dock was still being built. He called his crew to pick him up. It was later that evening when Dean received a call from a strange number. He knew she would call, and he was waiting for her.

She told him earlier about her tiny cottage and that she might need a backup plan. Jess said, "If I tell you the address, you must then promise to me that you know nothing about where I'm located."

Dean promised he would keep her secret. Dean picked up his cell phone and said, "Hello, Jess."

"I'm fine. I'm at the cottage. A small tourist shop hired me. There isn't a diamond in the store."

She gave him the address and phone number of the shop and her new cell phone number remained in the recent calls slot on his phone.

Dean carefully mentioned, "I can either bring your new identification cards or mail them."

"Mail them to me, please."

"I would like to see you every now and then. Maybe I can pick you up in the new helicopter and take you for a ride on my new motorboat."

"I need a little space right now and time to think."
He understood. She never mentioned Derek or asked about him. He guessed that subject was taboo. Maybe they could discuss things like love later. He knew to let Jess have space and make the next contact.

"My condo is placed up for sale. Moving closer to the Los Angeles area would be easier for me to visit you. As soon as I know the new address, I'll let you know. I also need a little space right now."

He could hear her smile over the phone.

It was hard to break away from Dean for a short period. He was her mentor and guide. Friendship with him was easy and always would be. She swallowed and hesitated. But then she said, "Talk to you later." She hung up.

Dean called his real estate agent and told him to drop the price a little on his condo, as he was anxious to leave the San Francisco area permanently. Jess said she would talk to him later. He was glad she still wanted a connection with him. He would help her.

He was glad she trusted someone. The communication line between them was open. He should have warned Derek.

Dean knew her problems with trust issues. She was so like his daughter. Both women flew solo, unafraid. He would have to tell Jess about the eagles. They flew in pairs.

28   The Cottage and Mary

THE SMALL TOURIST shop manager placed a sign in his window, and in blew this young hippie lady by the name of Mary James on a small dirt bike. Mary looked around and there wasn't a diamond in the place. Mary said, "Perfect."

She told the manager she was renting the cottage a mile from town and needed a job. She wore very black tight exercise pants, a crochet top with purple push-up satin bra underneath, leopard leather thongs and matching small handbag with a thick black fishnet strap with huge brass pulley type buckles. Mary didn't tell him about the small gun in her purse.

Her hair was some unknown color with streaks of purple, and her yellow hoop earrings swung when she talked. Her sunglasses were barely moved from her eyes.

Mary explained, "I'm very good with numbers and a cash register. I dropped my identification card in the water on the boat ride over and the duplicate should arrive shortly. You can copy it to check me out later."

The store manager liked this girl, lots of spunk. She also wore purple bras just like his sexy wife who made him a sandwich every day. She didn't want him to go to the restaurant across the street. Too many pretty girls were there.

After filling in the application, Mary asked, "Where is the Propane Company and Hardware Store located? Also, is there a local boat rental place nearby?"

The store manager always paid his workers in cash. Then he could fudge on his return, and he wished she would start the next day. He liked to have at least two people in the store, but it was okay for her to take her one-hour lunch break any time she wanted. She just needed to coordinate with the other person. If there's an emergency, it's okay to just lock up the store and leave.

A week later, the fake duplicate identification card arrived in the mail, and she let the manager make a copy. The copy went in the file, no check on employee was ever done.

Mary saw Dean whenever he could make it to her little town. She thought about Derek, but never mentioned his name to Dean. Dean knew she was hiding all her feelings inside. He decided to wait things out. He knew everything worked better with time. Being good friends was important.

One weekend, he moored the boat in San Diego, and she agreed to see his new motorboat. He picked her up in the helicopter and landed on the moored boat. She was impressed. She loved the new boat and took the third bedroom. They went shopping and Dean bought her some new clothes to leave on the motorboat.

He wanted her to feel like it was her home away from home like the sailboat had been. She could stay on his motorboat any time and whenever she wanted. Dean didn't tell her that he saw Derek once a week. He was surprised, but he truly liked Derek. He was one of the good guys who needed a friend too.

XXXXXX

Derek looked everywhere for Jess with his secretary also working the system for him. He checked with her art galleries. There were no new photo pictures. She turned in photos of Point Reyes and Tomales Bay. It was painful to see those photos with the soft light. He thought of her standing, there taking her shots. Whenever she sold a painting, the money went into an offshore account. There was no trace of her. She vanished just like the chameleon salamander guy and was off the grid.

105

He liked the fact that Dean moved to Los Angeles, and he occasionally dropped by for a visit. Derek would talk about some of the cases that he was on, but the conversation eventually led to Jess. He really wanted to go there to talk about her and what a screw up he'd been.

Dean knew Jess's dreams. She wanted to live in an African diamond mine and dig for the stone. She wanted to go deep sea diving and find buried treasure. She wanted to move mountains and save someone. Jess had visions. She talked about tigers and what kind of motorcycle should a person buy. She wondered about race car drivers and were they good people. She talked about a snake woman that she thought she saw. It was her visions that she kept private. Dean had a hard time figuring her pattern of thinking.

He knew that Derek would have to hold on for the ride if he wanted Jess. There was something out there hitting her radar screen. Derek would need to be wide awake to capture anyone wrong in her path. That was the picture that Dean saw. Derek could protect Jess. That would be a good thing. He believed in the young investigator's abilities and her insight. Dean saw the two people that he very much loved; they were dancing together on a large boat deck. It was their future. He believed their love for each other was a possibility. They needed to drop the floodgates and combine trust into positive strength. Dean would try to mitigate a meeting between the two by dropping a clue. He knew they had a shot at love and beating the criminals. He would bet on the odds. "Oh, yes, every time!"

Dean played his part. He knew how to help them build a good life. Patiently, he waited for a time to slip the information, and the moment gelled before him. A man wanting sat in his condo. Dean listened to Derek for an hour and then moved to his bar to pour himself a large drink. It was hard for him to listen to the re-hash of an event in the past. The boy was stuck. Dean was trying to help him. He didn't look at Derek, but would look at the ocean out of his huge Los Angeles condo glass window. It was a glorious day outside with heavenly blue skies. Maybe today, the young man would get the picture. Dean hoped so. He took a big sip of his drink, and said, "That's too bad."

This was the sixth visit. Dean repeated and did the exact same thing every time. His repetitive words and actions seemed odd. Derek did a retake in his mind of the previous meetings. It suddenly hit him that he knew where she's currently living, of course. What was it he told me a long time ago? Like a daughter. What was the one word, magical, she was *magical*. She is way ahead of the normal brain. He's all the way into helping and standing by her. Standing by her is something I failed to do. Dean was loyal as best he could. He's been trying to help me.

Dean saw the recognition go off in Derek's eyes. "Smart boy, after all."

Derek would now call Jim to tail him, and Dean smiled. Derek quickly left the condo and called Jim to meet him at his apartment.

XXXXXX

In all these months, Mary arranged everything in case she needed to escape quickly. She received via a special mail courier some fireworks from Dean's friend with step-by-step instructions written in a shaky hand. She learned how to rig the release of propane and to set up the blowing device.

She became acquainted with the young teenager who was renting the boats on the island on the side for extra money. He shared his dream of wanting to leave this island. Mary shared with him a loose fact, something about having a different name called Anna Taylor, and the likelihood that person was an undercover agent. He now must keep her secret.

The boat boy was fascinated by her. Sometimes she would give him a quick hug and kiss. Boat boy wanted more. She would always smile and said, "Not yet."

Boat boy could wait. She bought him a cell phone. It was so she could call him anytime. She told him to always keep the boat gas tanks full and that phone charged. He filled the tanks every night and plugged in his phone.

Mary also hired a hooker on the next island to do a special job not quite ready yet. The hooker worked at the local bar by the boat dock. Mary bought her a cell phone. She would call her when the plan was ready. The hooker liked doing nothing and getting paid for it, so she would be ready when needed. She kept her phone charged.

29   Finding Mary

DEREK ASKED JIM to track Dean's helicopter trips. Dean mentioned to Derek that he was doing a lot of flying lately. Dean flew to a small airport five times and the rest of the locations only once. Jim went to that airport every day and sure enough, Dean's helicopter landed again.

Dean picked up his rental car and drove to this small town with Jim tailing him. Dean stopped across the street and walked toward a small tourist shop. In five minutes, out walked Dean with Jess. They ate at the restaurant. Jim recognized her hand movements immediately.

Jim said to himself, "Good, good disguise. I love the purple satin push-up bra. My camera's going to take amazing shots. He would give anything to see Derek go berserk after he sent him the photos."

Jim had to stop and laugh. The first photos he took were side shots, and then Jess looked his way. He was far enough away with his super camera lenses. He zoomed in and took a perfect close-up shot.

Walking over to the tourist store, he picked up the store's business card. Jim picked up a small box with a green fishing lure inside. The orange stripes on it caught his attention. The lure was a little faded from being in the store window. He wet his finger and smeared over the lure. The thing absolutely did glow. Jim was satisfied.

He figured that he better act like a tourist so the clerk would give him information. He also put a candy bar with the lure for good measure on the counter. The bar was one of those peanut nugget things that he hadn't eaten in a long time. Come to think of it, he hadn't seen them in a long time. He looked at the wrapper for an expiration date. There wasn't one. "Oh, well, how bad can corn syrup be if its old?"

The clerk handed him his bag of goodies. "We don't sell too many of those candy bars. The young people don't like them."

"Those kids probably wear braces. The corn syrup sticks all over that flimsy wire and makes them look like Halloween teeth." The store clerk giggled. It was the reaction he was waiting for. He politely gave her Mary's description and said that he wanted to see her while he was in town. The store clerk was super friendly to the customers, wanting to impress them with her knowledge of the town and its people. She knew exactly where Mary James lived and gave him the address. She didn't know Mary's cell phone number though. He asked the clerk not to tell Mary because he wanted it to be a surprise. The store clerk promised.

"If you need more nugget bars, come back and see us again. I'll have to tell my friends what you said about the bars and corn syrup. That line is a really good joke."

It never amazed Jim how some women could turn into a walking, chatty doll. He tried to remember what he said that was so funny.

"Will do. You have a nice day."

Jim drove out to the tiny cottage, which stood in the middle of nowhere. There was a single old oak tree approximately fifty feet from the house. The store clerk told him the cottage was real old, around since the terrible slave days. He didn't drive down the small road leading to the house. A person never knew who was watching, and he didn't want to raise suspicion either. He also saw the propane tank. It was a huge mother sucker for such a tiny building. Jim's brain was being polite. There was a better description for the tank. He remembered a French word, "couillon." That tank was a couillon for sure and threw him for a loop. He didn't see any other buildings from a former time to warrant such a huge tank.

He took photos of the cottage and later shots of the tourist store. Jim ate his sandwich and poured himself a hot cup of coffee from his refilled thermos. He dipped the candy bar in the warmth, softening the corn syrup some. "It's not too bad."

The weather was nice, and he rolled down his window while he thought. After eating half the bar, he threw it out the window and was surprised a large vulture swooped down and picked it up.

"I guess the vulture doesn't care about expiration dates either."

Getting back to his dilemma, he liked Jess a lot and worried where he should place his loyalty. He had known Derek a long time. Jim trusted Derek with his life. He transferred the images to his phone. Slowly he pulled up all the photos one last time. Something told him not to press the button. He was reminded of scam e-mails that chewed up the data on your computer. They were thieves, stealing your software and personal information. Jim figured he was getting too old to do the investigator job. His nerves today were a little off. He looked again at the cottage trying to feel any bad vibes. He didn't feel them anymore. He sighed and reluctantly hit the send arrow to route the photos. Derek and his secretary would receive them, along with the address and location. The only name on the file was "New Lead--Mary."

Derek received the photos and went crazy. He paced the floor and ran his fingers through his hair. He worried that he wouldn't have any hair left if he kept stressing out over Jess. His secretary canceled his appointments the next day. He would be on vacation the next day and possibly the next. Derek put his own disguises on and rented a car. He started driving at night and reached the small town by early morning. He went into the restaurant for breakfast. He just finished, and in walked hippie girl.

The girl, Mary, glanced his way, smiled, and then picked up her apple bagel and latte coffee. She chatted with the pretty restaurant girl and laughed. She glanced at her huge purple leopard plastic watch on her wrist and took a bite out of the bagel with cream cheese oozing onto the wrapper. She walked out of the restaurant humming to herself.

Derek was fascinated. Jess was a wonderful undercover actress. He realized she was not afraid to change her life. She was doing a great job of protecting herself. Jess didn't really need him. She could live without him. That was another solemn fact he must face. He needed to touch her, hold her once more. He wanted to kiss her soft mouth. He missed talking with her. She was always interested in his day. He wanted to be in her world.

Derek picked up the newspaper to block his unhappy face as she exited the store. He drove out to her house and stayed on the road quite a while. He remembered his last words, *I wonder why I'm even here.*

What a stupid remark? He should have told her his fear that he couldn't protect her. He should have told her he loved her. Derek wanted only Jess. He messed up. He wasn't sure how to move forward. Derek thought he lost her. If he approached her now, there would be no open door. She turned off all her feelings toward him. She didn't trust him anymore. Sadness entered his soul.

He slowly turned his car around. *She would be safe there for a while until he could think up a better plan*, he thought.

Derek drove back to Los Angeles.

The Salamander rented an apartment in the same building as Derek's secretary. He briefly chatted with her in the halls when he took out the garbage. He visited her apartment several times. He asked for her help with his computer. Sometimes the secretary would show him how to do it on her home computer. She accessed her work from home and she used this special code changing thing. She locked the device up constantly in her safe.

She didn't tell him where her safe was, but he quickly found it. He just needed her safe codes. He thought of the poison but then thought it was too risky. He kept talking to her about his favorite things. She would talk about her favorite things. When she was at work, he would try to get in her safe for the special key code.

Tonight, she came home happy, saying they found something important at work, a lead they were trying to find. Salamander took a chance. He began formulating a plan for this weekend.

30   Cottage Blown

THE WEEKEND ARRIVED, and the Salamander took secretary out for fried chicken dinner on Friday night at some cheap local restaurant. Once back to her apartment, he told her he wanted to show her something real funny that he found.

Secretary let him in to her apartment, and she felt a slight prick in her neck before she went down. It only took about an hour to get the safe codes. Secretary was half in half out under this new experimental drug his friend gave him.

Salamander gave her just another shot of a different sleep juice. He pulled the code machine out of the safe and was immediately into her work e-mails. It took him all night reading them and found a file from Jim Michaels. It's a lead file. He looked at the photos. Looked like her, but it wasn't her.

Who was this person? He would check it out. He undressed secretary and put her robe on from the bathroom hook and put her on top of her bed covers. Then he put everything back the way it had been. He remembered to remove the two small syringes.

He checked the apartment one last time and left. He didn't know by opening the file, the date and time changed. The secretary knew her files and would bring up the notice to her boss. Plus, she saw some slight bruising on her neck. She always bruised easily.

Salamander headed to Mary's small town, and it was night. He drove out to her cottage and unscrewed her porch light. Then he knocked on the door. He was under a new disguise, of course. There was no one home, and a full moon was out. He would have to wait until morning. He drove by the tourist store; nobody there either. He parked his car down by the hardware store until morning, catching a little sleep.

Mary held her camera carefully, shooting the moon and mist pictures. She felt lonely and melancholic. It wasn't the same after knowing Derek in Napa. A part of her heart disappeared. Even her photographic pictures appeared flat. That was all right. She hadn't submitted any of her new photos to a gallery, afraid they would trigger her location. Now the moon shots might work for the gallery. They held some mystery, as if her feelings transferred into the photo.

Her heart was eternally warring with her feelings. If she originally went to the cottage and hadn't tried to rob the Napa Jewelry store, she probably could have lived there at the cottage. Having met Derek again changed things. Memories of his face and love kept entering her brain. Derek was always in her thoughts and she knew those thoughts would stay with her forever. Out in the moon-lit night, there was no denying her feelings for him were strong; the bond sealed tight. She had tried to keep up the actress-mode of not caring, but Dean saw through her.

Dean casually mentioned that love sometimes was hard, but therein lied the reason it was so valuable. It was more precious than all the diamonds and gold in the universe. People that didn't devote themselves to the concept were always lost. Dean made her smile when he said, "The loveless are those ghosts that disappear in the night due to lack of gravity. We should be glad that we are not ghosts." She remembered the ghost restaurant in San Francisco.

"I am not a ghost or a robot. I feel and love."

The escape plan she made didn't fit anymore. It was fun for a while, but she was tired of living some character's next movie. The movie madness ended, her part played out. She wanted to step back into reality. She wanted to be held again by Derek.

Putting her camera equipment away, she still definitely felt part of the lost. What if Derek had moved on? He had every right to do so. Mary sat outside for a long time, hugging her knees until the moon became smaller and drifted further away. It was an emotional reckoning with herself about her beliefs and needs. Time away had helped her heal and get a new perspective.

She arrived back at her cottage and checked the front door. Someone opened the door while she was out because the thin translucent nylon was broken. She pulled up the images on her security camera. The wires were hidden behind wood board trim she had placed on the house with a new octagonal air vent that hid the camera. The photos were dark. She went out to the front porch, and someone loosened the light bulb. She went back to the images and tried to lighten them.

Unable to recognize this person, she felt a creepy feeling. It dawned on her that the Salamander found her. With all her careful planning, the monster was here. There was nowhere to be safe. She must go to Dean. The motorboat would shield her. Dean would help and guard her. He was the only person she could trust.

Mary went out and dug up her things that were in plastic boxes in the yard and stored them near a safe boat pickup location. She called boat boy and the hooker to be ready the next morning about nine fifteen for boat boy and nine thirty for hooker girl. They would be ready.

Mary was bailing. The next morning, she would have to go to the shop which opened at nine. She forgot her backpack with the extra camera lenses. She would just use the back door of the shop.

The next morning, she set her timers on the fireworks display and the timer on the propane tank. It was her property. She had fibbed about being the renter. She could blow it if she wanted. When she bought the place, she submitted a written request for a permit to demolish the tiny building. She did forget to mention exactly how the demolition would be done. She just would maybe need to pay the fireman's bill.

Looking one last time at the inside of her cottage, she saw the small kitchen with wood shelves and the old white stove that was missing the bottom. After reviewing her real estate contract, she had noticed the house and its contents were: As Is. At the time, she thought this piece of information was fine. When she inspected the stove, she said, "Go figure." She had thought as is meant working still. It was her mistake in not understanding the clause. She realized her cooking skills were a match for the stove, like in nonexistent. Jess had contemplated buying marshmallows to cook in her fire-pit stove, but couldn't find long enough sticks on her property. There was the oak tree, except the branches were too thick. It was too soon to start a bonfire, so she bought a small microwave. That solved the stove problem. There was an old rug and soft sofa chair in the living room. No bedspread adorned the roll-a-way. She used a sleeping bag. The place would look better without the building. She believed the real estate value of the land would increase. She shut her door and made sure it was tight. The key was thrown in the field. There was no need to keep it, even for sentimental reasons.

Mary hopped on her bike and steered toward the tourist store. The store opened, and Salamander was talking to the store clerk. Mary arrived and was in the back of the employee room. She knew his voice. It was the same voice from Napa. She heard Salamander.

She didn't need to see his disguise. She remembered correctly. Hopping on the scooter, Mary shoved it a distance from the shop before starting the engine and drove toward the boat docks.

Climbing in the boat with boat boy, he mentioned they must hurry because there was another client who wanted to leave the island. Mary asked him the description of the new client. It was the same guy that was at her door last night.

Mary calmly left a message for Derek where Salamander was located.

The boat arrived at the next island dock. Mary waved to the hooker who came down to the dock. Mary introduced hooker to boat boy and left the scene. She gave boat boy the keys to her dirt bike to keep forever because undercover agents always left stuff behind. It was the expense that happened in that type of business. It was his lucky day.

She picked up her rental car and turned the vehicle toward Los Angeles.

Mary called Dean to pick her up at some rental place in four hours. Outside the cottage, the sky was suddenly filled with fireworks display in broad daylight, and the propane tank rose thirty feet in the air on fire and landed on the cottage. There ensued a huge bonfire that even Mary could see on the next island.

Mary laughed, "Take that you freak reptile, my version of hellfire."

She stopped on the road, took a picture, and sent it to Dean. Receiving her note, Dean had fits of laughter knowing she was safe or would be shortly.

Talking with his secretary, Derek listened to her explain strange bruising on her neck and how the Mary file was reopened by someone. That's when Derek received Dean's note. Mary was safe, and attached was a photo of the burning cottage.

He checked an unknown phone message, recognized Jess's voice, and quickly called the island police to hunt down Salamander. Jess tossed the phone, so Derek couldn't reach her.

He sent the police to his secretary's apartment building. He found a new apartment for his secretary that afternoon. Salamander already left the island with a different boat boy. He escaped the police easily. The criminal mind worked the game well.

Derek called back Dean at his condo and the motorboat, but he already left to meet with Jess at the agreed pickup location. He didn't answer his cell phone either when he recognized Derek's cell phone number. He needed his concentration focused on the unfamiliar roads. Roads disappeared when you flew unless there was a required emergency landing.

Jess told Dean, "Run silent, run deep, lock everything down, do it magically." Dean would follow her instructions. Jess was more important. His loyalty was solid. Dean didn't even need to stop and think about who's side he was on, like Jim had.

Dean knew Derek was running into extreme complication with Jess. He worried that Derek was not strong enough. Harv hadn't worked out when Dean introduced Jess to his lawyer. Harv messed up royally somewhere with Jess. Those facts didn't surprise him in the least. She had thrown Harv out of her life. Dean also had found a new lawyer when he moved to LA. He had thrown Harv out of his business, except one small warehouse in San Francisco. Dean was smart in keeping one option open. The warehouse didn't cost him too much to maintain.

He pondered and hoped Jess hadn't given up on love entirely. Derek wasted time and let more miles develop between them. Dean felt that the man should have approached and talked with her at the cottage. Derek let their differences become more important than true love.

Being her strength and support right now, Dean would be her protector for as long as he could. Dean was a huge fan of true love. Jess loved with heart and passion. He loved her free spirit love, but then he was old, easy to know the game of love. Dean loved Jess back with everything he had. Dean bet on passion every time. Now passion was real. He knew it was no secret, heart led to passion. Love was that simple. Loving heart with heated passion always worked.

"How to bring Derek onboard to simple?"

31   After the Cottage

DEAN AND JESS were on the new eighty-five-foot boat motoring toward Catalina Island. They planned to moor there for a while. They had been further south, but decided it was time to move the boat. Jess pushed her blond long bangs under a headband to hold them. The hair was back to her natural color with no trace of purple. All the hippie clothes were gone.

It was about two weeks since the cottage blew. Her tan next to the bikini was looking good. She felt better and was rested. Dean's phone said he was out of his office on vacation and to leave a message. There were many messages from Derek. Dean began to feel sorry for the guy. Now his phone said his message box was full.

The two of them talked about the pretend wedding plan again and both agreed that it was the only way to go in the future to capture Salamander. The Salamander was fixated on Jess. They knew that Derek must be brought onboard to the idea to capture the reptile.

Jess wasn't sure anything in their relationship was going to work. She also didn't quite know how she felt about Derek. Her emotions kept going back and forth. She wondered why he hadn't tried to find her. If he cared, he could have tracked down her location. Maybe he did find her and walked away. Doubts invaded her thoughts. Had he even said he loved her? She was reluctant to see him again. She told Dean that piece of information.

Dean got up and fixed himself a drink and said, "That's too bad."

"No, that was good. It was always better to stop a relationship in the beginning."

Dean knew Derek was still in trouble with Jess. "How much longer would it take Derek to find the motorboat? Perhaps I ought to invite Jim for a drink on Catalina Island. I miss my good friend, Jim Michaels."

Dean went down below to make the call. His helicopter was temporarily off the boat. His pilot was taking it in for a tune up. The boat reached Catalina Island and dropped its anchors. Jess went down below to shower and change. Her shower contained a button to turn on music and Jess pushed the button.

Dean saw the police helicopter coming. "This is what a person would call perfect timing."

Jim and Derek exited the helicopter and it flew off again. Dean pointed down below, "Third bedroom, in the shower."

Derek headed below deck.

"Got any booze on this tub."

"Welcome aboard, Jim," and Dean pointed toward the bar. "Nice big green lure on your hat. It matches your pale eyes. It looks extremely like a lure that I saw in a tourist shop a while ago."

Jim looked a little sheepish.

"No matter where you bought it, I'm glad you came for a visit. You're always welcome. I do believe our young friends will be gone for a bit. Is the police helicopter new? It's very shiny. There's a football game coming up on the TV monitor shorty. We both should enjoy it."

"Boy, this is the life. You have a television monitor out here. That's neat!" replied Jim.

"Isn't it now?" Dean found the clicker and tuned in the game. He was glad that he made the call.

Derek found the third bedroom, went back to the lounge, and grabbed two glasses, champagne, and opener. Then he quickly moved back to the bedroom and locked the door. Jess was done with her shower and opened the door to get her towel.

Someone grabbed her arm and pulled her out of the shower into their arms. It was Derek. He was kissing her all over and feeling her body. He felt good, and she wanted. It had been a long time since she saw him. He wanted her more than anything. There were miles of difference between them.

Their time the past months were lost. The distance was too much, but the heat and fire of love burned in their souls, melting the hurt partially away. Clearly, their relationship in the sexual world was always good. Heat enveloped the two strangers, placing the world on the outside.

Surrounded by passion, their bodies entwined like before things went wrong. Differences melted into dust. Love held the two lovers, carefully embracing and encouraging them to find common ground. Common ground encountered real love. Real love reigned for a while until they were released from its hold. Their difference of opinion was another story. It would try to pull them apart.

She let him feel her body and carry her to the soft bed, enjoying the familiar heat. She let him make hot love to her until he was finished. Her world began spinning. Then she calmly moved out of bed, the other differences still existed there. "Where are the important words? You haven't said them."

She grabbed her robe, and headed to the lower lounge taking the bottle and her glass of champagne with her. The wall between them was there. Derek exclaimed, "Unreal." He felt the wall. This was not going the way he planned. Jess was the most complicated woman he ever dated.

He dressed and went out to the lower lounge with his glass. He could tell by the way she was sitting that she was still mad. Derek said, "How's your day honey? More champagne?"

Jess glared at him and started laughing. "We have to talk. There's a wall."

"Yes, we do, and I feel the invisible thing. I don't want it there between us. Can we go back to the first day we met and start over? It was the best part of my day."

"I don't want your controls anymore. That was why I left. I'm my own person with important thoughts and desires. You treated me as if I don't have a brain."

"I'm sorry. I know you're smart. There's never any question about your intelligence. I'm struggling with how to protect you. I feel that I must do that very thing at all costs. You must understand my viewpoint."

"I will try to understand. Your constant protection mode needs to relax and go on vacation."

Dean and Jim heard the laughter and raised their drinks to each other. The boys turned back to their TV program and the game.

Derek and Jess joined the two men on the upper deck. Derek poured himself a large drink and sat in the lounge. Jess sat on a stool by the bar wrapping her bare feet around the bar stool legs. She did that when she was stressed. Dean understood things were still not good.

"Hey, everyone how about we eat?" He ordered the chef to bring out the meal.

Derek informed Dean that the pretend wedding set up was on. Dean and Jim were surprised by that revelation. It was a point in their plans that had been stopped by Derek. He was now willing to work with them to catch the bad guy. Jess won Derek over to that concept. She tried earlier with Derek and failed. It was a major shift. Dean made a call to his accountant to set the airplane and special taxi arrangements to take them to the chartered airplane in two weeks. They were back in the game.

Jess left the lounge to go further up to the main bridge of the boat. Dean turned to Derek and motioned for him to follow. Derek shook his head and said, "She wants to move slowly."

Dean shook his head, "Well, at least she didn't say stop. The door is open, man."

Both Derek and Jim turned in for the evening. His helicopter was scheduled to return after breakfast tomorrow morning. The helicopter would return Jim and Derek to land. Derek sat long enough and headed to the bridge.

Derek found Jess sitting on the curved cream-colored upper lounge of the bridge area, looking at the moored boats in the lit harbor. He approached her and kneeled in front of her and put his head in her lap, holding her. "I'm sorry. I don't want to be on the opposite side of the world from your love ever again."

Jess touched his hair and he moved up. "I'm sorry. You're an important part of me. Without that part, it hurts. We both have hurt. Truce, no differences anymore?"

"We stomp the crap out of our differences and throw them into oblivion. We do it together because we have time to build our dreams. I will give you a thousand truces and more."

He lifted her off the lounge and held her in a warm embrace. He whispered in her ear, "I love, want, and need only you."

She smiled. He said the important words. They kissed and slowly began their familiar touch zones. Derek took her hand guiding her to the third bedroom down below.

Jim returned to the kitchen area for a bottled water and saw them. He went to Dean's door and knocked once. Dean smiled and knew, "Not moving slow anymore."

After having eaten a scrambled egg buffet the next morning, Jess and Dean waved the two men and helicopter off the boat. Derek waved at Jess in her red tank top and tight white pants. Derek thought, *my girlfriend looked like the Point Reyes Lighthouse, a beacon in the storm. She is my light.*"

Jim smiled and said, "It's a good day."

"Definitely a magnificent day. Early mornings are always the best part." Derek knew to keep things simple from now on.

32   Pretend Wedding Setup

THE FOUR OF them took various taxis to get to the small airstrip in case they were followed. The chartered jet quickly flew them to Las Vegas, Nevada. Dean checked into the luxurious hotel as Mr. X with his team.

The hotel welcomed Mr. X as if he was an old friend, giving him one of their luxurious three-bedroom, three-bath penthouse suites, which overlooked the vibrant city. There was a mini bar with kitchen, large living and dining area, along with an outside balcony of lounge chairs. The balcony was accessed through huge sliding glass doors. Jim checked the bar, and wasn't surprised that it was fully stocked. He wondered if they had any peanuts.

The bus boy arrived with their bags. Another hotel person arrived with a large bouquet of flowers followed shortly by two chilled bottles of champagne, delectable chocolates, large fruit basket, and luncheon meat with exotic cheese tray, olives, and caviar. There was a large basket of salted peanuts. Jim was delighted. Dean couldn't help but notice the huge pile of nuts on Jim's plate.

The hotel concierge appeared and personally handed Mr. X the invitation for this coming Saturday night's private poker game. He mentioned the players were listed inside the card. Mr. X reviewed the player's names and smiled. He nodded and said, "Yes, my friends would also be side guests to the party." The concierge nodded and left the four alone.

They sat in the dining room plush roller white leather chairs, ate the appetizers, and chilled champagne. After choosing their rooms, they adjourned.

The scheduled meeting was set at two in the afternoon to initiate the pretend wedding setup. Their plan was called Jumpstart.

The large motorboat was pulled out of the water and would be retrofitted with guns, special netting, underwater gear, cameras, and spearfishing equipment plus motorized underwater jet machines. There also would be huge spotlights, night scopes, disappearing doors that held hatchets, knives, and more handguns, rifles, flair guns, etc.

Special high-powered Jet Skis and pop-out flotation rafts were also installed with mini-motors. Shark repellent and guidance devices as well as survival gear were fully loaded on the rafts. Additional radar was reengineered to temporary police computers and additional onboard computers.

Dean ordered the stuff when Mary first moved to her cottage and set up the installation date. He planned on doing this anyway, but now the police were paying for some of it. The police worked on the underwater net and divers.

Most of their meetings started with, "What if?" At their two-o'clock meeting, Jim brought up, "What if he brought drones?" Dean wrote down, "Need sharpshooters and make sure spotlights rotate three hundred sixty degrees, and any additional night scopes."

Dean explained that all the boat charter places would be monitored for that day and evening. The police set up a special trap location to catch the suspect as any charter boats would take the Salamander there.

"What if he steered his own boat?" asked Derek.

"Special operation helicopters would track that vessel."

Dean's cronies found their own special trap location in the next cove from the police trap. Their cove was chosen for the single road that led towards the mainland from the beach. There would be an open dune buggy and wires. The cronies checked out their system with a straw dummy, and it worked. They had fun with the second dummy and put some grey feathers in the head. From a distance, it looked like hair. Some of the boys wanted to try out the second dummy, but it was getting late, so they went home disappointed. The cronies also set up their own escape boat and a special signal. Only Dean knew about these plans and the cronies, of course.

Their meeting was over, and it was time to play. Jim and Dean went down to the noisy casino for some roll-the-dice action. Jess and Derek were going to a show later, so headed towards their bedroom for a nap. The young people couldn't leave the room fast enough.

Dean asked Jim, "Do you believe that idiot nonsense about a nap?

Jim had a twinkle in his eye when he said, "Let's get some broads of our own for the evening so we can have some different kind of conversation."

"I already made the call and the lovely ladies were waiting downstairs for you and me."

"Perfect. I like forward-thinking people. I know you've made our arrangements. And thanks for the nuts."

They all met each other again at nine thirty for dinner and, after dinner, called it an evening.

33   Working Jumpstart Plan

ANOTHER WEEK PASSED by, the four of them continued onward with the plan. The poker game was a blast for the side spectators to watch the elderly gentlemen play the con artist games using their minds to lay down their hands.

On the casino floor, Jim lost, won, lost, won, and lost his money at the games and tables. Jim was at exactly zero, right where he started. Everyone teased him that the gods were not working in his favor. Dean won three hundred thousand dollars in the poker game. Jim told him, "It was dumb luck."

Dean bought a Fancy Violet Gray two-carat diamond ring and ten-carat Fancy Violet Gray diamond necklace. White diamonds surrounded each carat stone and the setting was platinum. Dean explained, "I can write the jewelry off as a business expense because Jess would wear it for the photograph with tuxedo-dressed Derek to entice Salamander to the wedding party." Jess loved the ring and necklace, noting that Dean only bought the very best. Those diamonds cost a huge amount of money. She knew her diamonds.

Derek and Jess met with the photographer the next day. Jess looked stunning in her strapless white sheer dress and diamonds, as did Derek. They looked like a beautiful young couple in love. The photographer captured their passionate hearts.

The photograph and article about date, time, and place of wedding reception were put on hold until they were ready to release it to the papers and media. The article would contain facts to read that the upcoming bride had been gone for eight months on a world cruise, just to confuse Salamander to wonder who the Mary person had been.

The next meeting, they talked about the abductee possibilities and devices to track and protect, such as special shoes designed with a knife and hook, special hair barrette for guidance tracking, and special ring that sprayed a mist to blind the eyes. There was also a bracelet that contained wire and a special watch with voice and microphone function.

Then Dean mentioned the worst scenario, "What about capture and inability of abductee to protect themselves in case all devices are removed? From the police profile, the Salamander was the type of killer to use possible rape and torture."

Derek got up and left the meeting, heading out to the patio. Jess looked at the two remaining men, "I'll talk to Derek."

Jess sat on the lounge and took Derek's hand. "It won't get that far."

"How do you know that?"

"Dean would blow him up or out into the water with the special hidden guns he was having mounted on his new helicopter and night scope. He also hired a person to fly at night, and he's taking lessons. It will be all right. He won't let anything happen to me."

"Then why did he bring it up?"

"Because he wants you to have a level head and be prepared for all scenarios. Dean pointed you in that direction so you're at your very best game when they encounter the reptile. The game is always to capture or kill the Salamander. Dean is reminding you of the final objective. His solution is to kill it, because the reptile is not worth saving. It's evil personified."

Her logic made sense. There was a reason why they decided to create the think-tank. It was to find any errors in their plan. Derek didn't like it, but knew this whole plan was going to be tough to implement. He needed to step back from seizing up whenever he thought Jess was in danger. His inaction or ill-preparedness could be disastrous. A cool level head was required every minute once the plan went into action. He looked at her hand that she squeezed. She was ready to get with the group again. Jess was, sometimes, unstoppable. He was the train wreck happening. He must get a grip. This was what he was good at, catching the bad guy. That's all this creep was, another very bad guy.

"A reptile was just a reptile." He mimicked Dean's words. Jess knew Derek was back in the game.

"Full throttle ahead?" said Jess.

"Absolutely, let's run the creep into the ground." The two went back into the meeting.

The men were continuing to strategize. The bucket of chicken, rolls, mashed potatoes, gravy, and spinach/orange/bacon salad had arrived, and the players took a break. Jess grabbed a cold bottle of water and had a horrible vision. She placed her fork down and stopped eating. Derek noticed. "What is it, Jess? You look strange. Is there something wrong with the salad?"

"No, it's something that I saw briefly in my mind. It may be nothing."

Derek knew that with Jess, nothing meant that he needed to dig a little deeper. "Go on, we would like to hear what you have to say. We've been on a roll with ideas."

Jess sighed. Her idea was worth tossing out. "The men should also have the special gear. Salamander may take one of you. Then my loyalty to one of you would force me to meet with Salamander. He knows all of us from Napa and would have control over the game. The reptile is devious and always thinking about capture methods. His mind twists quickly and he grabs onto objects normal people wouldn't think of using."

All three men looked at Jess. They hadn't thought of that avenue of destruction by the creep poisoner. The scene she painted was a scary one. Dean broke the silence and said softly, "Smart girl."

Dean wrote all the equipment down. He explained it would take an extra week to get the additional gear. Everyone agreed that another week would help their people ready any further preparations.

34   Hitch in Jumpstart Plan

SPECIAL TUXEDOS FOR all the cronies were ordered with a special stripe on the side of their pants and the outfit was the same for the waiters so that they would appear as waiters. Special cell phones would be given to them.

The Land Department checked out any special caves in the area and sealed them with heavy wire. They had to respond to a hysterical chicken farmer that was missing a couple of gray ducks. The chicken farmer blamed them because they had been in the area. None of the employees of the Land Department knew anything. The police figured that the eagles got the ducks. Guards were installed in the three men's apartments/condos in case the Salamander decided to do a cave-hostage upgrade. Jess's special red dress was ordered.

It was now four weeks since the four of them met on Dean's boat on Catalina Island. Jess ran out of birth control pills when she was Mary at the cottage and didn't want to get a prescription as Mary in case the doctor would check her background. She bought new birth control pills as Jess when she arrived back in Los Angeles, but hadn't started taking them until two weeks later.

This was after Derek made love to her when he yanked her out of the shower and again that evening. Jess was over a week due on her normal menstrual cycle which was always exactly on time. She quickly talked to Dean on the outside patio.

Dean hugged her and made a call to a local female doctor in the area. Jim went off with Jess to the doctor under the disguise of shopping. Derek was all right with the shopping expedition as he was working the police end. Jess came back, and Jim left her alone with Dean.

"I'm most definitely pregnant."

Dean contacted a former police woman he knew in San Francisco that left the force and looked a little like Jess. She would do the switch due to the amount of money Dean offered. Dean already made plans for a special closet in Jess's room on the boat.

The woman took the same size dress, so a second dress was ordered. Dean ordered a larger pair of special shoes. No problem, the company could easily do that pair along with the rest. Jess didn't want Derek to know just yet. She said, "Derek was a wreck already and would go berserk if he finds out."

Both Jim and Dean were happy to let her call the timing of that shot of news. Dean and Jim were excited and talked about giraffe stuffed toys, tiny fishing outfits and poles, and babysitting grand kids. Jim's schoolteacher friend was good with her grandkids.

Derek returned and knew something was up but couldn't pin anyone down to talk. Every time he walked in the room, the boys stopped talking. Jess had enough scotch for the day, which was unusual. She drank a small amount of white wine instead. They ate dinner together and listened to one of the fantastic singers perform and strolled back to the hotel.

Derek and Jess's lovemaking was off the charts, and all Derek could think of was getting married. He didn't know if it was the proximity to her every day or the atmosphere surrounding Las Vegas. It was a perfect place to get crazy. But then, he already was long gone about her before he arrived.

He proposed the next morning, serious, but knew she would put him off. She didn't put him off, however. She gladly accepted his proposal when he said, "I've loved you from the first day we met. Or was it the second day? You're the only real thing that happened to me. You're not pretend anything.

You're major important in my life. You're my only desire. We can build so much together."

"I love you major as well. There's never any pretend, not even the first day when we met. Lots of differences of opinion, but I know they're of minor importance. Our pride and tempers get in the way. We're both strong in many ways. I want to be strong with you. Living and building together is what I want. I'm glad you feel the same passion. I'm happy and ready for our journey to begin."

They started a heart-to-heart discussion about family and kids. He wanted lots of children. Jess wanted to think about only one child at a time. It was the perfect opportunity for her to divulge her secret, but she let the moment pass. She was still assessing the discovery on her own, trying to grasp the changes that would come to her body. She would tell him later when the timing was more appropriate. She didn't want any disruption to catch the poisoner. The poisoner may have the necklace. Derek made the marriage arrangements, unaware of circumstances surrounding his soon-to-be-bride. There were still trust issues between them. That tension would eventually arise.

Two days later, Derek and Jess snuck off to the little chapel with her hidden white dress and tied the knot. The next three days, they were so giggly and locked into the bedroom, Jim and Dean entered their room when they were out for a walk. Checking their luggage, sure enough, rolled into a scroll in Jess's backpack was the marriage license for Mr. and Mrs. Derek Wright. Jess always put her valuables in her backpack.

Dean ordered huge bouquets of white flowers and a three-tier white gourmet wedding cake with lemon filling, which was delivered with five bunches of white balloons. There was champagne, white wine, or sparkly fake champagne, caviar, and oysters with chef-made crackers. There also was special pasta with warmed vodka meat sauce in case anyone was real hungry and Caesar salad for Jess. He hired a string trio to play the wedding march when the door was opened and later during the party.

When they returned from their walk, they were greeted with the real wedding party, not a pretend one. Derek and Jess were photographed a second time by the photographer that Dean brought into the suite. They would have a photo book to remember their celebration. Dean and Jim bought them their first Christmas silver ornament engraved "Just Married" as a small gift.

Dean and Jim moved to a different room for two days to give them privacy. They ordered room service, chef-designed meals for them as an additional gift for two days. They were given a bag of Vegas chips to play at the roulette tables if they were bored.

Dean gave Jess a credit card to buy honeymoon clothes, and the two men were glad that was over.

True love conquered and brought peace.

35   Final Jumpstart Plan

PLAN A AND B were complete for the protection onboard and outside the perimeter of the motorboat. The four were sitting at the dining room table for their final wrap-up meeting. The motorboat would take three more days before it arrived at the boat dock. Dean was excited to be back soon on his beloved motorboat.

Jess frowned and said, "What if Salamander hired someone else to do the first job for him? It would be someone who was close to build, height, looks, etc. It would be someone as off the rocker as he was. It could be someone, male or female, who provided him with the poison. The police will catch the fake psycho killer like they did with the fake diamond necklace. They don't know right away the person was the fake. But it was enough time for the Salamander to escape free. He was free to then do the real job when they will be unaware. The Salamander becomes the great con artist in his mind. The group will be left exposed to his hellfire-poisoned mind, all caught in his trap. I believe we need a Plan C for the con artist in case it takes place."

The three men stood, went to the bar, and Dean grabbed the orange juice. The other two men fixed themselves a drink. The time was early, only eleven o'clock in the morning. They sat back down at the table and talked at once. Dean said, "No way, but definitely a possibility. Totally believable. This killer is slippery."

They were running out of time and needed to capture every little possibility where a psycho would move in the world. It was after all, just a creature, not human. If anyone encountered the creature, they would not recognize anything as human. They all agreed. The Salamander was inhuman, and he must be caught.

Their net of plans must be extensive, with backups beyond the normal. Extra crew was needed for the massive backup plans. If they didn't cover everyone, the creature could escape. They agreed that everyone must know about the harm this creature could potentially wreak upon the world. There must be no surprises. Everyone must have full knowledge, so they could prepare their known sphere of help. The police couldn't be everywhere, but the crony world could.

Jim said, "I'm in for a Plan C having seen this same scenario."

Derek said, "Jess is out of all the plans. I feel she's not protected in any of our scenarios."

Then Derek paced and went berserk. The two older gentlemen looked at Jess and she shook her head, no. She hadn't disclosed her pregnancy.

Derek didn't yet know about the baby. He only knew about Plan C. The two older gentlemen relaxed because this situation they could clearly handle. The food trays arrived, and they all ate. Derek calmed down after looking at a determined Jess. Overly protective wife protection was not what she wanted.

He sighed because she was too smart. She was locked into catching the bad guy who wanted to hurt her. She was also too brave. Jess was a warrior. Derek remembered the picture of the blown cottage and her totally calm phone message saying that the poisoner was on her island. She had given him the coordinates from her very terrific and known guidance device.

Derek figured that message loud and clear from the Tomales Bay incident. She wasn't letting the bad person destroy her life anymore, so she was dissecting his every thought and move. She wanted the bad guy out of her life. Derek wanted him permanently dead. There would be no conscious concern in his brain when he pulled the trigger and emptied his clip into the man or any of his cohort's in crime. Jim, Dean, and Derek were on the same page as were members of the crony team. He nodded to Jess they should continue. He was on her team on every level. Derek hummed a tune to his favorite opera song. Jess smiled. It was a sweet memory between them.

The four of them worked on Plan C. Decisions were made where all the players might be in that situation and the number of crew still required to catch the thief.

Derek went off to a conference room to meet with his superiors, who brought their wives to Las Vegas. The wives were out spending money as fast as they could for their very dressed-up evening and special entertainment show. They were going to enjoy their night and could hardly wait.

36   Pregnancy Revealed

THE PRETEND WEDDING motorboat party was a little over one week away. They returned to the Los Angeles area. Derek stayed the night on the motorboat with Jess. Dean and Jim were top deck.

Jess and Derek saw the breakfast buffet covered trays ahead of them. Jess pulled the cover off the one tray and saw the habanero sausages and said, "No to that item." Then she lifted the second tray with a strange-looking squid thing. She put the cover back on and said, "Not that one either."

The next tray was stuffed cow tongue, and Jess fainted upon seeing it. Derek dropped his plate and caught Jess before she hit the floor. He yelled for Dean and Jim to help.

Jess awakened to the three men looking at her. "I forgot that you're not fond of the last dish my chef prepared. I could have the chef make some oatmeal or something else if you want. Maybe dry cereal would be good. No, you like the warm stuff. I would ask my chef to make some with brown sugar and a few fresh blueberries."

Dean chuckled because he knew it would make her faint. She hadn't told Derek about the baby yet. Dean and Jess argued over that important fact.

They helped Jess stand up, and she ran for the bathroom and upchucked last evening's late-night snacks and soda. Derek looked at Dean and Jim. They knew what was wrong.

Derek felt stupid. "What's wrong with my wife? She's pregnant."

The two old gentlemen saw the lightbulb go on in Derek's brain and sat down on the lounge waiting for the show to begin.

He went into the third bedroom and started hollering at her. Derek ranted, "Are you an absolutely crazy person to put yourself in that much danger? That guy would kill you and our baby. Of all the lame things to think that you can catch this guy and be pregnant at the same time is some nut job. You're not normal. Who would be that brave? No, who would be that crazy? Nobody. You're in the realm of the beyond. Can't you for once ask me for help? Why can't you do that one simple thing?"

"Oh, no, wrong way. Here we go again." Dean was alarmed, because the two people were there before. Jim also was concerned.

"I was going to tell you, eventually. Now, I'm not going to discuss anything with you. I'm angry. You should go stuff your antiquated, overly protective ideas somewhere else. Try parking them into oblivion." She felt guilty that she hadn't told him sooner, but she wasn't going to admit that slip. He should have been nicer to her. Her temper was churning as was his.

Derek stormed out of the bedroom, helpless as to how to deal with his strange wife. "I'm going to just kill her. It would be a lot easier."

That's when Dean grabbed him and calmly said, "Sit down *now*, idiot father." He knew that Derek would never hurt Jess, but the man was being irrational. He could understand his frustration with the wife. Jess meant well, but this time he was on Derek's side. A man likes to be informed before his wife faints before witnesses, even though those witnesses were good friends. Jess's timing in telling her husband of the pregnancy had taken too long. As a friend, he must help them both to see the real picture, which was that something special would be happening in their future life. It was also important to always keep a pregnant woman from getting too agitated. Mother bear could hit the rafter any time soon. One thing about women was that they changed weekly. Derek needed to recognize those concepts real soon. It was time to someday have a heart-to-heart talk with Derek, if he wanted to. First, there was this problem.

Derek sat down as that word hit him like a ton of bricks. He needed to breathe. It wasn't Dean's use of the word now, but it was the other word. He was going to be a father person. That was a dad. He was pregnant. No. Jess was the one pregnant. He and his wife were having a baby, a real live baby. He didn't want to go to oblivion. He went there once and was on the outside.

Dean almost started to feel sorry for him. Jim had been there, so he told Dean to move cautiously. Dean knocked on Jess's door.

"Jess, darling, it's perfectly all right to come out."

Jim brought the six-foot-tall stuffed giraffe animal into the lounge. He placed it in the center of the floor. Jim and Dean decided if the stuffed tongue didn't work, they would have to move to plan TFB--The Fuzzy Baby huge giraffe with an embroidered sign on the neck registering the words, "Boy or Girl." They knew Jess was reluctant to bring up the topic with her husband.

Jim and Dean did think she was being a little female crazy from screwed-up hormones. Those hormones did weird things to a woman.

Jess commented, "The giraffe is rather cute."

Derek snorted and jumped up to fix himself another plate of food. He brought juice and the cracker basket which were handed to Jess as a peace offering. Then he bent down, kissed her hair, and sat down next to her. He held her hand.

Derek said to her, "I'm going to be a father. We would be good parents together. I'm sorry you don't feel good. I love you so much. All I wanted to do was help. You must know that. Truce."

Jess smiled because he said the important words. Derek loved her and was trying. She needed to try asking him for help. She needed to include him in everything. She had placed him on the outside and that was why he was upset initially. She must stop that type of action in their future.

Dean pointed out that huge fact to her. She must trust Derek with her whole heart. Dean knew she loved Derek. If she loved him, they must fly as a pair. She knew Derek loved her. They would make good parents. She could fly as a pair with Derek. She would try.

Jim and Dean were glad that stressful incident was over and done. The two old men breathed a sigh of relief. The rest of that day was pretty much calm. Both new-to-be-parents were looking at portable cribs on the computer that would fit on the motorboat. It was good to hear their laughter. They knew it would be a quiet night.

Later everyone heard the number six calypso song on the intercom. Dean and Jim hit the Silent button. Dean informed his crew, "Stand down, lovebirds learning the calypso." The crew knew the dance song and moves so there was no problem.

Dean removed the Silent button, because he also liked the song. He knew the stereo would roll and play the next song, number seven and then stop. He really liked seven best. It was about darkness and moves and babes. There were words about winning and losing, which reminded him of Vegas. The crew let Jess and Derek own the deck.

Jess was teaching Derek to dance her queenly nymph song in the moonlight. He was learning fast. He always liked to watch Jess move. She danced real sexy, sultry like a vixen tempting him. Derek didn't know this song or this wife. It was a totally new experience to him. The music was rocking his center of gravity once more.

He twirled her carefully as if she were a precious flower in his hand. She felt soft and her hair smelled good. He wanted to be the one person with the goddess on her island. The steel drums sounded their electric music in tempo with the fast beat. The dance was rocking side to side, a give and take, back and forth, and repeat.

Derek could balance gravity and do the earthly dance. She was bending toward him. He caught the mythical, desirable woman. He was her prisoner. Derek loved the song, and he loved her.

37   Plan D–Death to the Con Artist

IT OCCURRED TO the group that now they needed a Plan D. Everyone agreed it would not be a good idea for Jess to be anywhere out of either of the three men's sights.

They couldn't trust that the Salamander hadn't somehow wormed his way into the cop network. Dean knew he could trust his old friends, and they would heavily guard her with the three guys' help. With the boat fully armed, they thought it was the last place the Salamander would appear.

They felt confident this was where the inexperienced imposter would appear. They also didn't think he would come near the boat because of all Dean's cronies. Salamander didn't want to get tangled up in that underworld mess because the fence guys' network reached to Canada, Mexico, and Miami.

So, they developed the Plan D for "Death to the Con Artist." What was the matter with the Salamander? He developed a thing for Jess because of the diamond necklace that really belonged to her family. The Salamander killed people to possess the necklace. Somewhere in his screwed-up mind, he reasoned why he must finish his kill of Jess.

Jim told everyone the story of what happened in the cave when he called him, "piece of crap." The psycho jumped up and down, screaming. Jim thought to himself that this guy had buttons he could push to his advantage. The psycho came over totally calmed down, studying Jim as if he were some lab rat specimen. Psycho spoke, "Where is she?"

Jim played dumb, "She's over there in the chair, and you're a psychobabble piece of crap." Jim had pointed to the schoolteacher. Same thing happened, more jumping up and down.

Jess said, "So the murderer is real sensitive and doesn't want to look stupid. He wants to appear to the world as smart. Therein, lies his weakness."

Derek said so the setup for Plan D must be the very best con artist job ever to trap him. If we trap him, he would go crazier in prison. Prison would lower his image to its weakest state. Jim and Dean agreed. It was a game of the conned doing the con artist in. Jess began to wonder if the diamond necklace was worth all the chaos. Perhaps the necklace was the bad luck.

The former police woman, Tami, would be used for Plan D as her experience gave her the edge. She was given her red dress and all the technical weaponry. She styled her hair the same as Jess.

The pretend wedding party was on. All the police were on board for Plan D. Extra old cronies were hired in case the Plan D police failed. The extra cronies from Miami were best friends to one of Dean's best crony friends from San Francisco.

There was a marker favor owed and the Miami cronies were glad to repay the debt to the San Francisco cronies. Payment would close the books on that subject. Dean's cronies assured him that the Miami group was one evil killing machine if need be. Dean told his best friend crony that he always kept extra sums of cash laying around just in case of an emergency.

That fact was relayed to the Miami cronies who brought extra men and equipment to Plan D understanding code language very well. The Miami cronies even went out and bought a small padded delivery truck. They had experienced this game before.

The final piece of Plan D was the release of the wedding photo to the newspapers and media. The ad was large enough. People could see the beautiful couple and her diamonds. The impending party date, time, and location were included in the release. The release also included a note of gossip to the media, which was speculation that Jess might be pregnant. She possibly would attend the motorboat party later in the evening, staying off sight. They weren't sure when she would arrive, other than she would be wearing a designer dress. The group thought those two pieces of information would make Salamander go crazier and create confusion. The confusion would cause him to align into their final plan.

38   Pretend Wedding Party Evening

NOW THE WIVES of the San Francisco cronies got together with the Miami cronies' wives and insisted upon coming to the party. They all ran into each other at Pierre's Designer Boutique in Paris last year and developed a solid friendship, sending each other e-mail messages over the network.

One of the San Francisco cronies' wife found the wedding invitation in her husband's pocket. Those women also had been around the block before and knew how to handle themselves. The women were real familiar with unsavory people and guns. The women invited the very independent Miami wives to the party. They were strong women who thought alike. They could be useful to help Dean's new friends. They also saw the gossip about Jess wearing a designer dress. Who wouldn't want to see the dress? They certainly did. There was no way they were going to miss this party unless there was a massive flood or hurricane to stop them.

The lead crony in San Francisco contacted Dean and explained the situation. He wanted to know if the wives could come. Dean told them it was all right, but the women must wear something red, just a small piece of red so the cops would know not to shoot them. Dean sent his friend sixty-five more invitations. He was glad he ordered the bigger motorboat.

Now after that phone call, Dean thought this party was going to be interesting. He cancelled sixty-five of the actors that were hired. The fake imposter killer was one of the actors canceled and wormed an invitation out of one of the onboard team of waiters. The waiter group now consisted of fifteen people.

All police, waiters, actors, Dean's people, and everyone were in place when the cronies and their wives began arriving. The women hugged Jess and knew right away she was pregnant. They talked to her about the wonderful baby stores they knew. It was a grand boat party--noisy, loud, great food, gourmet wedding cake, champagne, wine, beer, and lots of appetizers and huge chunks of men-type slices of meat. The photographer was an ex-cop and took lots of pictures.

As the party was winding down, imposter killer got his syringes ready in the bathroom. The solution he had was fast-acting and temporary, not the killer juice. The other guy carried the lethal package. The bathroom camera caught a photo, and it was sent electronically to the awaiting police on their monitor screens.

The watch was initiated on waiter boy. They weren't sure if he was a junkie shooting up or a killer. They needed to hold and monitor him. Information was relayed to Derek, Jim, and Dean who didn't let any waiters close to Jess, glad the cronies' wives surrounded her.

Jim noticed the photographer moving closer to Jess. He knew the guy and never liked him. Jim was surprised that he was on the list of cleared people. Jim motioned to Derek, who was close to Jess.

Derek saw the photographer approaching. It was hard to tell if the photographer was trying to get closer for a better shot. Derek looked at the high-powered zoom. There was no need for him to maneuver closer. Derek reached for his weapon.

Meanwhile, one of the San Francisco cronies' wives kept getting jabbed with a tray by this nasty dark, greasy-haired waiter. She kept an eagle eye on the waiter guy. She wanted to get closer to talk to Jess, the beautiful bride in her designer red dress. Wanting to know the designer's name so she could buy one, she felt inspired. Her husband was checking out that dress all night. He also liked her shoes as he kept staring at the red satin platform heels.

Jim recognized there were more than one imposter and held up two fingers to Dean and Derek. The cronies saw the hand jester, and knowing the signal, palmed their revolvers under their jackets, getting ready. They noticed Derek reaching inside his jacket.

Things always broke at the end of a party, known fact. Everyone wanted to have a nice time first before the fireworks started. The women also knew the gestures and got their purses ready. Something was going to break soon. The police were suddenly alerted to everyone's posture and movements. The tension was high.

There was no fear in any member at this party. Dean said to himself, "Hellfire starts about now." Dean alerted his people.

Jess saw the photographer and knew he was the imposter. The photographer licked his lips, and she noticed his eyes. They were glazed, and his pupils were huge. He was hopped up on something. She saw the syringe in his camera hand the same time Derek pulled his gun out and pointed in his direction. All the cronies drew their guns and aimed at the photographer. Dean and his guys watched waiter boy.

Jess used her hands to motion to the ladies to get down. Jess and the women fell as one except the red dress crony's wife. She was watching waiter boy. Derek and the cronies take their shot as the photographer bent toward Jess with the syringe extended outward almost touching her. The camera fallen to the floor forgotten.

The many single fired bullets brought the photographer down, the syringe falling to the floor. The cronies were expert marksmen shooting once a week at the gun club. It was their time to socialize without their women around.

The waiter saw the damage and ran to escape. The red dress crony's wife used her body and purse in a block-tackle move spinning waiter boy into the water. Waiter boy popped up like a cork with his waterproof gun. He commandeered one of the cronies' boats with a crony driver who knew which cove to take this perp.

The crony driver flashed the boat light once, exclaiming to stupid waiter boy that it was a battery problem. Dean and his boys saw which boat as did the cronies, and they all smiled, "Dead meat, straw dummy worked just fine. We'll see a dead man driving our rigged dune buggy shortly. Wish we could see those gray feathers explode."

Jess and the other ladies were fine. The red dress crony's wife could ask her question. Jess told her the designer before Derek whisked her out of there. Dean and cops covered the dead photographer's body for the removal team.

Derek moved Jess safely down below and started kissing her all over. She did a great job getting the ladies down. She told him the ladies talked about the maneuver and tried the same routine after their yoga class. He needed to call his waiting superiors and told her, "Later."

"She would be ready for any Plan C."

"Derek and the others were getting ready for Plan C."

39   Plan C & D Final Outcomes

BECAUSE THERE WERE two killers on the motorboat, Plan C with a third killer or killers was imminent. Dean and his boys, Jim, Derek, and the police were ready. The cronies and wives saw a new boat of body guards for the wives arrive. Because there had been two, Jim held up three fingers, then four fingers, then five fingers. Everyone got the message. The next group of killers made it through the underwater nets in their scuba gear and underwater jet machines per the police. The police were closing the net in after them.

The motorboat was alerted. The designated shooters took their positions around the perimeter. The scuba guys were met with guns blazing from above a short distance away from the outer perimeter of the boat and couldn't get close enough to plant their explosives.

The fish in that zone around the motorboat became known as the dead zone. The fisherman couldn't ever catch anything in that spot as the bullets on the floor moved with each swell, scaring the fish silly that there might be another drop of the bomb bullets that had killed their fish friends.

The scuba guys moved away from the motorboat and surfaced waiting for their helicopter. They gave up on this project. Their helicopter knew the coordinates and flew to the pickup location. Their helicopter pilot picked up the scuba men. Flying away, the pilot saw Dean and his new helicopter with guns approaching. The police helicopters flanking Dean flew toward the rogue helicopter. The pilot of the rogue escape helicopter quickly moved to the location the police commanded he land. The scuba guys tried to run out of the cove, but were quickly surrounded and apprehended.

Now the former police officer woman was also a black belt karate instructor and won numerous medals. She met one of the Miami crony guy's son, Cortez, and they instantly got along. She told him she even liked Miami and went there for vacation every year. Cortez told Tami he would love to know when she visited, because he could show her lots of good fish restaurants that his family owned. The Salamander picked the wrong girl to mess around. She thought the stupid twerp should take cover. There was no fear in any member of the D Plan. They received the notice that they were probably next and should prepare themselves as Plan C had been foiled.

A fake salamander drove the pizza truck to the location given to him. He went to the motel room and brought the pizza for D group. All the cops and everyone knew not to eat the pizza. They already ate their gourmet pizza delivery courtesy of Dean two hours earlier. The empty boxes were stashed in a plastic bag in the closet.

The pizza salamander guy was arrested by the police. The police picked him up and handed him over to the Miami cronies who put the guy in a padded truck and took him out to the country to await Jim and Derek's arrival.

Jim and Derek enter the padded truck to visit pizza boy, who was handcuffed and chained to the truck. Jim approached the guy. Jim spoke, "Piece of crap." The pizza boy did nothing. Jim spoke again, "You're a psychobabble piece of crap." Still, nothing happened, so he said, "Not the guy." Jim and Derek left. Miami boys were disappointed and returned pizza boy to the police for further arrest.

The Miami boys received a call from Cortez. Cortez and the former San Francisco cop girl, Tami, were going to hit a dance bar that was close by. They thought they were done for the evening because of the capture of the pizza boy. Tami noticed the vehicle following them. She asked Cortez if it was his team. He told her the color of the van was wrong. Tami knew it wasn't her team.

Cortez called back his people and told them he thought he was being tailed by the real Salamander. The Miami guys sent him to the cop location next to the cove where the straw dummy waiter guy bought it. They believed this was the final real Salamander. The police were still at that location.

Miami guy's son, Cortez, also called all the other relatives not on the boat and gave them the very secret rendezvous location. His relatives grabbed their guns and headed towards the police cove location. Miami boys contacted Dean with the information and drove in that direction with the padded truck. They also contacted the San Francisco cronies in the next cove from the police to alert them to the real Salamander's possible destination. Convergence to one location would bring the episode to a conclusion, one way or the other. Survival of the Salamander was against epic poker odds. Dean and the cronies smiled. They would have started placing bets with each other, except everyone was too excited and busy. Stealth mode was required. They knew to run silent and deep.

40   Plan E - Elimination

PLAN E WAS elimination at all costs. Everyone notified approached the police cove location. Derek and Jim would arrive after the party was all over.

Salamander followed the red dress woman's vehicle, totally obsessed beyond the normal crazy zone. He moved from poison to eighteen-bulleted semi-automatics. He had not heard back from any of his teams and the record in his head was playing, Failure, Failure, repeatedly, driving him into a wilder state.

Salamander would kill the man and woman in the vehicle upon arrival. Jess should have let him take her to lunch in Napa. Then she would be dead. He was angry that he used all the stolen jewelry money and some of his own to round up this stupid team that accomplished nothing. He didn't need them because he was super smart.

Getting away with this kill would make him the great con artist. Then he could sell the diamond necklace that lay buried in Napa. He saw Jess in her dark clothes outside the jewelry store after the murder in Napa. They knew she was at the jewelry store to rob it. The two of them watched her. She tried to fool them. Jess was a thief like them. They wouldn't forgive her. Salamander was glad she didn't get a chance to rob the store, but her arrival curtailed their time to steal all the jewels. That was why they were obsessed with her. She needed to pay. They would make her pay. He was here to do exactly that, wipe her out. Vengeance was a good thing.

The two vehicles arrived at their destination, and the occupants exited the cars. There was no one else at this location other than crickets, so thought the occupants of the two vehicles.

The former San Francisco cop, Tami, mentioned to her newly found Miami friend, Cortez, about a situation exactly similar where she jumped over a vehicle to escape bullet gunfire. She looked at her new-found friend and said, "Escape to the back of the car." She pointed and nodded to him.

Cortez grew up with this type of action and worked at the gym specifically for such a situation. His family was big on preparation. The combined crony groups and police would take care of the evil one. They needed to get out of everyone's line of fire and fast. Cortez knew he was good at doing this, but was worried about Tami in her pretty dress and high heels. Tami wasn't worried about the heels at all. She could dance all night in them. The skirt of the dress was full enough and allowed her adequate room for jumping. Her muscle-toned body would deliver her quickly over the vehicle. He nodded, "Yes, he would be ready."

All the hidden cronies, relatives, and cops saw the point and nods. They all thought, *okay to shoot hellfire shortly.*

The Salamander grasped his big gun, feeling the cold steel barrel. He crazily believed his edge over the young man and red dress woman with their puny guns would win. The crazy person smiled at Tami. "You look different tonight but still pretty like I remember. I wonder why you didn't talk to me. I want you to speak. I love your voice. Perhaps you're afraid. I'm glad you're afraid. Your fear makes me stronger."

The Salamander missed his poison needles and syringes. He should have brought them anyway. He could have maimed them and then shot them up with poison. He could still do that very thing. He could pick up some large plastic garbage cans to put their wounded bodies in. There was tape in his car to keep them silent on the way home. He could keep them partially alive for days and slowly poison them. First, he would need to remove their clothes and accessories in case there were tracking devices. Removal of the woman's clothes made him more excited. He stared at the red-dressed woman. Red was the color of blood. What an interesting color? Salamander could make love to the red-dressed woman first. He smiled. No one would know. How could they know? Her body would never be found. "Brilliant idea." They would find the man's body only and wonder for years to come. Her husband, the investigator, would be frantic. "Oh, joy in that spectacle." Yes, that was exactly how things were going to roll tonight.

His frenzied mind worked overtime, clicking things off. The more the mind worked, the more twisted were his plans.

The scene was becoming creepy. The creep was mumbling to himself. She couldn't hear what he said, but she could guess. Tami felt the twisted creep want her. She saw his crazy smile. She thought his eyes looked like a snake in the wild. He was staring at her boobs. Fat chance that was ever going to happen. Tami had enough of the creep staring at her and enough of being a center of his focused snake eyes. She hated snakes and would have shot him if she'd had a larger gun. The blast would have sent the snake to the trees for the vultures. It was a nice image. Vultures needed to be fed. They were tired of birds and fish for a meal. She looked at Cortez and felt the man was strong. She liked her men that way and he was very good looking. The future looked very bright, indeed. She refocused on the current messy situation. Her cop instincts started kicking in. She knew how to do this action. The boys will take care of the creep. Follow the plan, girl, and screw him. "Tami, girl, you are very good at your job," she whispered to herself. She knew that was why Dean hired her. She was always calm under fire.

He looked toward the edge of the cove and saw trees. He used to hide in the trees when he was younger. Did mountain lions come down to the ocean to eat the dead fish and crab? He thought he saw a slight movement in one of the bushes. No matter, he could handle such a creature if it showed itself. He could handle anything. Salamander believed this was the perfect spot.

The police wondered if he saw their concealed, waiting bodies there in the trees. The cronies weren't worried. The reptile had unwittingly fallen into the police trap. There was no way the thing was leaving the area. Even the police wouldn't place a bet against the bust not going down. They were confident as their radios were on silence mode, and the sharpshooters were in place.

Tami could feel her heartbeat as adrenalin rushed into her body. She loved the rush. The creep was looking away from them. It was time to rock-and-roll. She gave Cortez the signal, and they jumped over the car, landing on the hard gravel ground.

Salamander turned to look at his disappearing prisoners, and then, sneezed due to the pine trees in the area. He forgot to take his allergy medicine. His eyes itched, too. When he was in Napa, he had to buy some over-the-counter pills which didn't work very well. He forgot to take his prescription pill for two days now. Automatic reaction to the pine made him sneeze. When he sneezed, he lifted his gun. It was the wrong move.

The two innocents were safe out of any bullet path. The blast of bullets brought Salamander down into a crushed heap in the bloodied dirt. The smoke and noise from the gunfire swirled around the cove. The mountain lions in the distance heard the racket and went deeper into the hills. Shocked seagulls and pigeons flew away into the blue sky. Their squawks filled the salty air with curses. There was no sound from the downed Salamander. The ants at the location hurried to reach the downed reptile. He landed perfectly on top their huge hill of sand.

The evil con artist's green-lensed eyes dried of all fluid, his cruel body riddled by a massive quantity of bullets, lower torso always to save the face for identification. All the cronies and relatives knew the self-defense rules when it came to guns. They were totally safe. Pictures were taken of the dead body when Jim and Derek arrived.

The identification process was completed. The man had brown eyes and wore green contacts. There was the devil tattoo. The police were happy, all the cronies were happy. Everyone was happy that the killer was dead. The poison killer, bomb person, and gun-toting wannabe villain was no longer a threat. The psychobabble piece of crap was dead.

The diamond necklace that belonged to Jess was still missing. There was no talking to the Salamander for its location and no evidence found in what they thought was his motel room. They had no idea where he had lived before arriving in Los Angeles. It was as if he didn't exist. The pizza boy and divers were hired through an outside agency who had never met the person who mailed them a check from Los Angeles. The police arrived at a dead end regarding any diamond necklace.

The missing necklace story was thrown out there to the cronies' wives to distribute over the computer networks. If they heard anything, they were to contact Dean.

Dean would contact Derek. Because there were no identifiable facts about the location of the necklace for a long time, they thought the necklace wouldn't be raised from the ashes. The diamond necklace appeared to have permanently vanished.

A man read the newspaper article about the death of criminals in a high police investigation in Los Angeles. He was not pleased.

41   Jess's Vision

JESS WAS NOW eight months pregnant, and sometimes sleeping was difficult. She left Derek in the third bedroom. He had flown up to the area to see her. She was with Dean in the Seattle harbor on the huge motorboat. Everyone thought it best to move the boat and Jess to a safer spot just to make sure everything was all right.

Besides, Dean knew some old friends in the area he hadn't seen in a while. Dean lived in Seattle many years prior and loved the area with all its islands. He really loved the coffee and fresh berries grown there. The seafood at the wharf was amazing and his chef was restocking their freezer with seafood and berries.

Dean took her to the Space Needle for a vegetarian lunch. Jess didn't want to cross the moving circle, so two of his crew lifted her over so they could enter the amazing three-hundred-sixty-degree restaurant. She kept scanning the view as Dean pointed out the landmarks he knew. She told him later she had a blast, almost as much fun as buying the calypso song in San Francisco. Dean loved it.

At two in the morning, Jess grabbed an ice-cold water from the galley kitchen and sat in the inner lounge on the leather couch. Soon Dean joined her having been alerted by a button in his bedroom by his vigilant crew team. There was nothing on his boat that escaped his knowledge. He hired himself the very best.

"What's up Jess?"

"It's dark."

Dean was now concerned. "What's dark?"

"My vision. I can't see him, but I know he's still there."

"What in the world? Who's there?"

"It's him. He has the same strange ring." Dean knew who she was talking about and was immediately on alert.

"I remember what you said about the ring. Salamander is dead. We found a body with confirmed identification."

Jess told him that she knew that piece of information.

Dean was more confused. "Who are you talking about?"

Jess was reluctant, and Dean held out his hand, He encouraged her to continue. Dean was her old friend. It was time to tell him. He would know what to do. She trusted him implicitly.

"I feel the same way when I arrived at the jewelry store in Napa at night to steal my necklace. I felt his presence first which stopped me. Then I heard his thoughts. That was the confusing part. It was part of the complex persons I thought of initially. They covered each other. The men were interchangeable, almost identical but not quite. They were twins. The second twin, this one that woke me now, was in the jewelry store that night, too. One of the men who saw me outside the jewelry store that fateful night was very bad. Of the twins, he was the greater evil. He was the real green-eyed twin. The other twin, Salamander, was the one that wore green contacts over his brown eyes."

Dean said, "No way."

She said, "Yes, way, definitely all the way to correct."

Dean jumped off the couch and told her that was unthinkable. Jess handed him the photo she was sent online by one of the cronies' wives. Dean responded, "This could be a fake."

Jess shook her head and explained to him. "I've felt the evil for some time. The evil is overwhelmingly strong now."

That was what awakened me tonight. "He's here in Seattle, the second twin with real green eyes. He's here right now and very close."

"Well, why didn't you say something sooner?"

She replied, "Because I thought no one would believe me. I didn't want to believe it."

Dean awakened Derek. Derek was totally in quiet-zone-berserk mode. He wondered how this new knowledge could be right.

"How did you know another con artist psycho person was alive and here in Seattle? I barely recovered from the last fiasco. I'm not sure I can do this again. A green-eyed monster is in Seattle. That's nuts."

Dean saw the doubtful look in Derek's eyes. Dean knew Jess longer than Derek and he believed her. Derek was sitting there wondering about her accuracy of information. Dean suggested they table the discussion until morning. He would get his crew to move the boat out of Seattle right now and head toward Portland. It was an easy thing for his crew to travel at night with all the expensive radar on the motorboat. His people picked up Derek so there was no concern about a rental car. Easy change on a different return flight for Derek.

Everyone could feel the boat surge forward. Dean wanted Jess to be safe and feel safe. He could see her relax, having expelled her vision. She headed toward the third bedroom with her water bottle lulled by the motion of the boat. She felt her baby moving and pushing. The time was close. She didn't think this baby was going to wait much longer. Jess would be relieved to get the birthing over and done. The first and end part of being pregnant were the most difficult.

Dean sat for a long time with Derek. Finally, Derek went to the third bedroom. He knew she would be asleep. He didn't want to talk about the poisoner.

Dean sat in his lounge a long time. "What did this second hellfire creature have planned?" Jess was no longer strong, but fragile with child. They must come up with a plan to shelter her. He felt on edge also that afternoon, probably picking up her distress.

The evil one saw the huge motorboat pull out of the harbor. He was upset that he hadn't arrived sooner. The man twisted his gold ring. Jess was correct--he had reached Seattle.

When the boat moored in Portland, they called the ambulance because she started having labor pains. Their little boy was born the next day in the early morning hours three weeks early, and Derek was by her side. The baby was just fine.

Both Jess and baby were brought back aboard the boat within three days of delivery with a retired nurse known by Dean's Seattle friends. She could stay for three months with them. Milk, diapers, baby formula, baby cereal, baby fruit, baby clothes, and blankets were purchased in Portland by his able crew, along with portable baby carrier, baby swing, bottles, and diaper bag. If they missed anything, they could always fly whatever it was on board the boat or helicopter and even fly in a doctor.

The baby was strong and healthy. Derek stayed with the boat two more weeks as they were headed south back to Los Angeles. The little boy was named Justin after Derek's father. Dean would help feed and change the little boy. The baby smiled at Dean and waved his hands when Dean spoke to him which was often. Dean told the little baby he sent engineered drawings to a toy manufacturer to make a motorboat just like his. They could play together with the divers and other paraphernalia on the toy boat.

Jess was taking time to heal. Derek continued to hold onto Jess at night quietly kissing her like they did when they first met. Derek held Justin a lot during those two weeks, too. Jim was notified of the wonderful birth and Jess's vision. The police were notified of the evil one's potential twin existence and new location. Dean notified his team and the cronies. The cronies notified all that they knew through their extensive grapevine of friends. News traveled as fast as the electrical charge in a hot-wired car.

42   Information on the Necklace

THE SAN FRANCISCO crony friend called Dean one day. The Miami crony's son and new wife (former police woman from San Francisco) heard a story about a diamond necklace from royalty that came up on the hidden underground market for sale. The price was three hundred thousand dollars (more than the price of the paste necklace fence job in San Francisco). The diamond necklace was for sale in Rio de Janeiro, Brazil, by some front fence named Julio Samba.

Tami told Dean that Julio was possibly this bad dude. All the local fences in the town didn't want to do business with the person because people always mysteriously disappeared. There were no body parts, nothing was ever found. The local fences called him War Julio, as any transaction with his group ended up being a battle at his horse ranch out of town. The local fences weren't that crazy about money, though; their lives were more valuable. So, the local fences didn't even tell their clients. But the problem with diamonds was that just the mention of that word perked up ears in all languages and levels of people. It was no different in Rio.

Dean debated about the information relayed. He asked Tami, since they were good friends, if she could obtain more information. She called him back. War Julio owned his horse estate outside of town close to the beach. There was a tiny, long strip of parking land owned by the city before the beach. The road ran parallel to the beach and was long enough to land a small airplane.

A person could see the estate house from the road. War Julio tried to buy the road, but the city officials refused to sell it to him as the road connected to the city Bird Sanctuary. War

Julio hated birds and hated the city officials. The city officials hated him right back and would look for any opportunity to throw him in jail. War Julio had a sharp lawyer who was always able to get him out on some technicality or obscure law.

She did not view the necklace but was told about the strange clasp. She would call her contacts to see if someone could get a picture of it with a cell phone without War Julio knowing about it. The Miami family knew some extended family in Rio that owned a maid service. Perhaps they could get into the estate house. She told him that the Miami people weren't afraid of anything in the world because they knew everything was disposable. The only thing needed was a padded truck, a few men, some guns, and poof. That made Dean laugh.

"I like the Miami family and am glad you bonded."

"The only problem was that the maid service might want a little extra cash due to the nature of this particular client."

Dean agreed that cash was always a good thing to have on hand in case some photo popped up on his cell phone screen. About one week later, Dean received the photo of the diamond necklace. The shot was taken on a bed with a close-up of the clasp. He specifically asked for that in his expense proposition. Now he must decide if he should show it to Jess.

First, he contacted his lawyer to ask him about all the rules, gun and boat laws, and permits that would be required to take his motorboat to Rio. He called his accountant to check on charter flights, asking him to make sure his passport and Jess's were up-to-date, hotels in the area, rental vehicles, small airplane rentals, and hired pilot names. He also the names of banks and to set up an account immediately.

He and Jess were currently on the motorboat in San Diego. Little Justin was now a year old. He thought Jim and Mary Beth could watch the child. The two of them moved in together and saw Justin all the time. Or they could take Justin, but he wasn't sure Derek would agree.

Dean needed to talk to Jess. "You may not want Derek in on the plan if you decide to go through with the purchase of the necklace. I know the twin of the Salamander could also be in Rio. If so, that would be our largest hurdle because I think War Julio is just another punk newbie fence."

43   Another Woman Murdered

DEAN AND JESS were on the motorboat. She showered and ate lunch. Justin was down for his nap. Derek flew back to Los Angeles.

"Do you still want the necklace?"

Jess looked at Dean. He handed her his cell phone with the photo image pulled up. Jess looked at the diamond necklace and immediately tears filled her eyes.

"I thought so. Now the price was three hundred thousand dollars in the underworld and the fence was a supposed bad one. The deal is in Rio."

Then he asked, "Do you want to invite Derek to the party?"

Jess got up and paced back and forth. She said, "If we don't tell him, he will surely kill me and possibly you. We just can't have that."

"No, we certainly cannot. Besides, we may need his help with the police contacts in Rio. Do you want to call Derek?"

Jess picked up her phone and dialed. Derek was driving the car to another location. There was a murder of a woman and the coroner believed it was from a poison syringe, as there were several syringe pricks.

"I'm on my way to a call. Can I reach you later?"

"The situation is that something word." Derek immediately exited the freeway ramp and pulled over. Jess sent him a picture of the diamond necklace.

"That's the diamond necklace, isn't it? How or where did you get it?" He scrolled the note down and saw the sender. "Put Dean on your cell, Jess."

"I must work this potential murder scene, and then I will fly down to talk with the two of you. I don't want you or Dean to do anything until I get there."

Derek arrived at the scene, and the smell of death was strong. The body was shoved under an old piece of broken cement slab at the dump. The bulldozer person noticed the extra amount of birds missing and vultures flying overhead. The weather had been cool, and the cement kept the body protected from the elements. It was a young blond woman in her late teens, who looked a little like Jess. There were several pinprick bruises on her neck and all up her arm. Then there was also a strange circle of pricks.

Derek turned to the coroner, "Junkie?"

The coroner shook his head, "Doubt it. Seemed to be poison."

Derek said, "Poison and so many pinpricks. The monster probably slowly killed her. The circle of pricks didn't make sense. Any identification?"

"None. The woman did have one visible tattoo. It was a tiny devil head, fairly new tattoo, under her wristwatch."

Derek asked the technician guy if they could move her arm a little, so he could see the tattoo.

"The tattoo is the same one Jess drew a long time ago and the same one found on the many-bulleted Salamander that the police captured. The small devil head was another coincidence, which was too eerie."

He told the coroner to let him know right away cause of death and, if poison, the type. Derek may have a match to another case. "How long do you think she's been dead?"

"Probably less than two weeks."

Derek turned in his report and flew back on an airplane to Jess and Dean. One of Dean's crew picked him up in his girlfriend's car. Derek said, "Thanks, man."

The crew guy said, "No problem. Always glad to do a favor for Dean."

"Dean will do a favor for Jess. Not only would Dean get the necklace for her, he would do it with guns blazing. Dean was probably already checking permits to Rio, so I better get with the program, or the two of them would go there without me. I know Jess."

Derek visited Rio before on a two-week vacation with this girlfriend from college who lived there. The girlfriend called him some nasty names in Portuguese because he looked them up after one particularly bad incident with her. Portuguese was the main language, so he was familiar with the territory and area. He also knew to drink bottled water and rent a moped, as parking was a problem with too many tourists. Derek didn't really want to go back to Rio. He couldn't think of any way to dissuade his very determined wife or her helper, Dean Crain.

"Now, there are two people very devoted to almost criminal activity. It will be my job to keep them out of trouble. With the two of them in Rio and possibly another psycho, that is a challenge." Derek knew Julio Samba. He also didn't want to explain that phenomena to either of them, but he couldn't see any way around his problem. The man called himself War Julio. Dean would have to visit the man's office at the estate in Rio and make his own assessment. Derek was still mulling over his past girlfriend. That had been a juncture in his life that he wished he could erase. Right now, he wished that he was in Tahiti or on a space ship to the moon. He had kept this information from Jess and now he was the person found hiding his secrets. She wouldn't be happy with him and he couldn't blame her. He had berated her many times for her secrets.

"God, help me!"

44   Decision about Rio de Janeiro

DEREK ARRIVED LATE on the boat and kissed Jess. Then he checked on Justin and gave his head a soft rub. He moved back to the lounge and brought a beer from the kitchen, sitting close to his wife.

On the drive to the motorboat, he received the call from the coroner. It was the same type of poison that killed the Napa area people and elderly woman from Los Angeles. The circular group of pricks were a massive dose of poison. He already made the call to his superiors that it was possibly the Salamander twin.

Before they talked about the necklace, Derek told them about the gruesome murder. "The DNA test hadn't come back, but he was confident the semen in the dead woman's body would be a close match to the Salamander, the twin version. It appeared she had been tranquilized many times with a milder drug before the person used the lethal dose of the circle poison."

Her roommate filed a police report. The police talked with the roommate, and she told the police the tattoo was new and her roommate, Susan Kamar, received the tattoo because her new boyfriend wore one just like it.

They wanted to know if the roommate had a picture of the boyfriend. The roommate told them she didn't like the guy who went crazy when she wanted to take both of their pictures together, so she snuck a picture and didn't tell either of them. Derek saw the photos. The dead girl, Susan, did look like Jess and the guy in the unauthorized photo looked like their Bill Barker, aka Salamander. It was close to the photo Jess had shown Dean and Derek in Seattle.

It was one of those times that he should have supported Jess and her vision in Seattle. He wouldn't ever not believe her. It was a hard lesson. Jess saw things. She was, somehow, in tune to the bad guy. Jess knew things important in an investigation. Her instincts were right on. She could be an asset.

Derek got up from the couch and chose a second beer and knew everyone was going to Rio. There were no more doubts in his mind. The bad guy had to go down. He would try to follow police rules, but if the man fell in the ocean, he wouldn't care. He knew Dean was on the same page. They were both lucky in that Jess had chosen them as her friends. He was lucky she stuck with him. Jess was holding Derek close and he was caressing her hair.

Dean explained all that he knew about the necklace in Rio and mentioned moving the boat and the possible help with permits from Derek.

Derek said, "I need to tell you about a berserk college girl I dated in Rio named Rosalie Pere. She called herself that name in college, but her real last name was Perez. I dated her for six months when she started calling me constantly. There was always something she wanted me to do or check out. She was really checking my whereabouts. I went on vacation to Rio de Janeiro to talk with her. I wanted out of the strangling relationship."

Jess listened fascinated by the story because Derek would never talk about the berserk college girl.

"This Rosalie was related to a rich cousin by the name, Julio Samba, or his professional name, War Julio. I know where the horse estate is located. I went there one time for dinner and met Julio. Rosalie adored the guy and his horses. War Julio was a little strange at first but seemed all right at the time. He did have bodyguards on the property. I know War Julio wanted to purchase the road in front of his property. He wasn't married when I was in Rio."

Dean shook his head, "Unbelievable coincidence, rather surreal."

Jess was shaking her head and wondered if they should leave the necklace in Rio de Janeiro.

Derek placed the call to his superiors. His scheduled meeting was late the next afternoon in Los Angeles. Letting them know about the police's approval and any assistance available would be known after the meeting. Derek decided to stay overnight on the boat. He hadn't wanted to ever tell her about Rosalie, but everyone needed to know the additional risk.

"Rosalie tried to stab me, because I wanted to break off our relationship. I tried to explain that she was a beautiful woman and could easily find someone else. That only made her angrier. She informed me if she ever saw me in Rio again, she would finish the job, not War Julio, but her personally."

Dean thought the situation was funny. Jess hadn't been the only one to give lover boy problems. He was impressed.

Jess, however, did not think her situation was funny. She would need to fix things quickly.

45   Diamond Necklace Set Up in Rio

DEREK HEARD FROM his superiors. He was going to Rio to help catch the War Julio fence for the city officials and catch the criminal poisoning twin to bring him back to the United States for trial. The police felt the diamond necklace would be a draw for the evil twin, or the evil twin was using War Julio as a fence to help sell the necklace. Or War Julio had purchased the necklace from the twin Salamander person.

Derek would be the investigator in charge checking the evidence. Derek called Dean. "Let's catch the creep in Rio and buy the diamond necklace for Jess."

Jess was also on the call on the speaker phone. Dean called his San Francisco connection to see if any of his Miami friends cared to tag along to Rio. Jim and Mary Beth agreed to babysit Justin. The motorboat headed south to the Panama Canal. Derek would be staying at the Palmetto in Rio and kissed Justin and Jess a temporary good-bye. He would fly back on occasion to Los Angeles. Derek flew to whatever port the motorboat was moored on its journey to Rio.

The Miami fences enlisted as part of the security squad on the motorboat and would fly to Rio when the motorboat arrived. They were very familiar with Rio and should be an asset. The Miami fence's son, Cortez, was on the protection team and brought his depressed, older brother, who needed a little excitement from his divorce. The divorced brother was the same age as the now divorced berserk college friend of Derek's.

There were always pretty girls in Rio. Cortez accidentally made that statement and now his wife, the former San Francisco cop, Tami, was coming to Rio. She knew men.

173

Tami's husband could look at the pretty girls, and that was it. She thought his brother could get him into trouble. Newly divorced people were on a high of their own. Their logic was a little off base from the rest of the young crowd. They were into party mode. That was why she needed to attend the protection team and any ensuing party. Consequently, some of the San Francisco fences were coming and bringing two of the wives who liked Tami. Jess was going to arrange lunch and let the ladies help her set up the estranged persons. She thought the two would have lots to talk about if she could get them together.

Eventually, the motorboat reached Rio and anchored in the protection of the cove with the boat within site range of the lush horse estate. All the players were in position and the fence meeting to purchase the necklace was also set up with War Julio. Dean would be the rich person who wanted to buy the necklace. His poker skills and crony skills were well known. His ability at keeping a straight face put him in the actor position of buyer, but he gladly volunteered anyway. Derek was pleased that they wouldn't have to use one of the local police. They thought War Julio could smell one a mile away.

Jess and the ladies planned lunch and invited Rosalie Pere or Perez. They brought the two Miami Cortez brothers along as guards. Rosalie and the divorced Miami brother got along beautifully and arranged to go moped riding the next day. Jess and the others saw the sparks flying back and forth between the divorced man and woman while they sat at the small restaurant tables.

Happy with the way her cupid skills managed to save the day, Jess let a surprised Derek know, "You're now safe."

Derek shook his head. "You're unstoppable sometimes."

The next day Dean drove with some of his protection team to the diamond necklace purchase meeting at the horse estate. The police were under cover at the Bird Sanctuary down the road listening in their disguise as forestry volunteers. Dean wore the microphone in his hat and hearing device in his ear like a small hearing aid.

War Julio didn't even frisk Dean because he was confident his gun people jumped at his command. Dean saw the diamond necklace and examined it carefully. The clasp had the ridge and he knew his diamonds. Dean motioned his guy to bring the money. War Julio raised his hand and said, "The price was now three-hundred-fifty-thousand dollars."

The cops were distraught by the increased price. Dean asked War Julio why the price changed because the diamonds in the necklace did not increase in number. War Julio laughed and rubbed his hands together. War Julio said, "Another American buyer wanted the necklace."

War Julio went on to further explain he purchased this necklace for a much cheaper price from this family in Italy who were bankrupt and needed the money. Their names were Renaliere and were once royalty. The Renaliere heir talked about two necklaces that were made fashioned with diamonds in platinum. The necklaces exactly matched, one was the grandmother's and the other one the mother's. The American buyer owned the grandmother's diamond necklace and wanted the matched pair. Mr. Smith told War Julio he purchased the necklace from this elderly woman and brought her a basket of tea and cookies as a thank you present afterwards.

Dean sat there and said, "A believable story. The family in Italy was named Renaliere who owned the beautiful diamond necklace and the competitor buyer owned the grandmother's necklace. The competitor wanted to buy the matching mother's necklace. The mother was still living. I might know the other buyer who's a competitor. I have a picture to show you. Would it be all right for you to view the photo?"

Dean pulled up the image on his phone that Derek sent. It was the other half of the roommate cell phone image of the Salamander's twin.

175

War Julio jumped up, "Yes, that's the other buyer, Mr. John Smith. That's the competitor buyer."

"Did he own a white car with super shiny rims or was he driving a red car? Was the license plate letters G-L-O-zero-zero-zero-zero?" Derek told Dean the San Francisco arrest story.

"Red car, but I didn't get the license plate number."

War Julio glared at his people who wrote down in a little notebook, "Get the license plate number."

"I unfortunately can't pay the price. When are you meeting Mr. Smith?"

"Mr. Smith will arrive tomorrow, and I'll meet with him."

The cops went nuts in the Bird Sanctuary when Dean said, "Well, if that deal falls through, let me know." Dean left quickly to move the motorboat out of view of the estate house and gave the information to Derek.

Derek knew the grandmother's necklace was the necklace given to Samantha, the mother of Jess. Mr. Smith had the necklace that was his wife's and wanted to purchase the other necklace. Derek thought they were close to unraveling the mystery and solving the poisoner murders. It was a long search on both subjects. He steeled himself with the final task at hand, catching Mr. Smith, the master poisoner.

Derek would talk with War Julio to bring him on board to the final plan. He hoped his prior relationship with War Julio would help. This was a game changer because War Julio could tell the police to go pound sand somewhere. War Julio was clean and was selling a legitimately purchased necklace, having produced for Dean the original copy of his sales receipt. Derek would have to appeal to his sense of fairness.

Rosalie once told Derek about a horse incident with a newborn colt. War Julio honored the contract terms when an owner died. He didn't have to comply with the contract for the valuable fertile horse juice, but he paid the widow the full amount anyway saying the colt was exceptional. War Julio didn't want to cheat the widow. Besides it would have been a mark on his reputation. That information from Rosalie was valuable.

46   Catch the Twin Con Artist

WAR JULIO WAS amazed to see Derek Wright walk through his office door. He loved his crazy cousin, Rosalie, but thought she was a bubblehead. He liked Derek and was disappointed by his cousin. He welcomed Derek back to Rio and wanted to know how he could help him. He was very glad to meet an old friend. "I also read the Los Angeles newspaper and saw the article about your marriage. How is your wife and do you live in LA? You must still be an investigator, yes?"

Derek explained his current problem and situation. Derek knew this was a very complicated decision. War Julio told Derek he enjoyed complicated. He also enjoyed the fence, Dean Crain. Dean was one of the interesting people on the earth. He would be honored to participate in the capture or destruction of such a low-life creature. War Julio had nothing better to do right now. Sometimes his life and business were boring.

Besides, his cousin mentioned Derek's wife, Jess, setting her up with this terrific Miami boy who owned a bunch of fish restaurants. He knew those fish restaurant owners. His sweet cousin, Rosalie, called War Julio and told him she might move to Miami. That was a nice favor. He did major business with the Miami Cortez family and their restaurants. They enhanced his business. War Julio felt he owed Derek a favor. Derek thought this was different. The gods were tipping the scales in his favor. He couldn't believe it. Their life had been torn apart by this creep.

Derek smiled--revenge was always sweet. Confidence in their ability to catch the evil one increased the odds way beyond the normal. He would share those facts with Dean. Then he would dance tonight on the motorboat with his valuable, exquisitely beautiful wife over her favorite number six calypso song. Her heartfelt gesture helped immensely. He felt like dancing. It had been a good day.

The next day, Mr. Smith drove his red rental sports car to War Julio's horse estate and stepped with his briefcase in hand toward War Julio's door. War Julio's people wrote down the red car rental license plate number. War Julio decided to help the police catch the American because then the city officials would owe him a favor.

War Julio was told about the syringes and knew not to get too close to the American man named Smith. The police showed War Julio a picture of the dead elderly lady, a young college man, a jail prostitute, and a pretty prostitute in Los Angeles. The police explained the man was a twin and both men had been involved in murder. War Julio was mad he killed the grandma with poisoned tea and cookies. He loved his grandmother.

War Julio put on his best poker face. Dean previously talked to him a little bit about poker and gave him the business card for the concierge hotel person in Las Vegas. All War Julio needed to do was mention that he knew Mr. X, and it was guaranteed that they would let him play. War Julio just needed to bring his money.

War Julio had laughed because he knew Dean was making a joke. Dean also told War Julio that he shouldn't worry about the road to the Bird Sanctuary because he could put in a small cement pad and buy a helicopter. Dean even gave Julio a card of an inexpensive helicopter manufacturer.

Dean sort of liked the young man. He reminded Dean of when he was younger. Dean was very good at assessing a man's character. That's why he had so many friends. Dean was a natural at conversation. He could talk to anyone and be best friends in minutes. I guess you could say that he had the "gift of gab." His friends were also loyal and stayed with him. War

Julio looked like he could use advice from an experienced fence. He looked like a young man who needed friends. He was also familiar with some of the Miami people. In the Miami group, there existed pretty women. Dean smiled. Should he introduce Julio to this one crony family's daughter? It might be an enjoyable show. Dean also liked to see sparks happen. This might be a good time to start something. If Jess could play cupid, maybe he should, too. Or he could mention the young man to the girl's father and put in a good word. The father would get things rolling in the romance world. His daughter hadn't liked any of the young men her father paraded across his compound in Florida. It might be a good time to branch out from home territory.

It was that sliding scale thing, again. There was good and there was evil. This young one was good. He could feel it. Dean decided he would win War Julio over. He talked about some of his journeys into crime and out of it. He talked about making money and his warehouses. Dean talked about good food and excellent wines. Both men were similarly cultured on those subjects. He talked about his boat and the adventures of flying. Next, he talked about women. That perked the young man's attention. Dean knew the man was ripe to fall in love. Oh, yes, Dean was going to help. There were always his annual parties. He mentioned a few of his parties and the fireworks show. War Julio was interested. The young man and his crew would get invitations for the next year's event.

Consequently, War Julio relaxed with Dean and entrusted him with additional information about the Renaliere family and gave him a brochure from an auction. There had been a painting at this auction he was going to purchase from the Renaliere's but didn't. At the auction was this other painting. It was another artist's rendition of a similar oil painting of the Royal Scots gray horses charging towards the viewer at the Battle of Waterloo. Only this artist painted the riders as North American Indians on the horses with war paint and arms raised with their bow and arrows. The painting was large, four feet by six feet and Dean saw it immediately. "Scary picture. The guy liked *Cowboys and Indians*."

War Julio liked Dean's reaction. The painting was purchased to scare people when they came to his office. It was really an image thing to keep people's respect. Respect was important and allowed him to do his business which was sometimes with unsavory characters. Dean would have put pictures of jaguars (the third largest cat in the world and good swimmers) found in the wetland called the Pantanal. The Pantanal overlapped into Brazil. Maybe those pictures were in War Julio's main home. It would be interesting to visit there, but not this time.

Instead, Dean invited War Julio to play poker in Vegas in the future. Consequently, War Julio shared more information. It was what Dean hoped would happen. War Julio shared the fact that he paid people to disappear, and the money helped to move his competitor's people out of town into his company. He needed good people to work for his ever-expanding fishing business in Curacao, North of the Venezuelan coast. The master chefs in the world loved his fresh fish. The fish business made War Julio a rich man. Dean nodded. Dean thought it clever of War Julio to abscond his competitor's people without them knowing. That meant the young man was a savvy businessman in his own territory.

Dean's next conversation included many years of deep sea fishing. The two men laughed about the gnarly looking creatures of the deep. They talked about the pacu fish in the Pantanal, which could weigh thirty pounds and had teeth that looked almost human.

ᏇᏇᏇᏇᏇᏇ

It was the day of the competitor meeting. Julio's trusted gunman wore the police wires and stood behind the desk with War Julio. Mr. Smith entered and was real nice and cordial. War Julio showed him the diamond necklace. Mr. Smith began to open his briefcase and paused. "Are you sure you won't knock the price down a little? Three hundred fifty thousand dollars seems a little high."

"This is the price for the necklace because I want to go to Vegas to gamble. I obtained a personal invitation guaranteed to Vegas. I also want to buy a new helicopter."

Mr. Smith contemplated his next action. He could try more conversation to bargain with the young jackass, but he looked at War Julio's body guard who kept looking upward. Mr. Smith saw the huge mirror. He thought it was a stupid place for a mirror and the Indian picture was part of the grotesque size of the furnishings. Even War Julio's desk was massive in size. The desk chair probably reclined so the man could look at himself. The man in front of him was trying to impress people that came to this office. He was some young warlord with his equestrian estate. He had heard the horses whinny as he walked to the door. That must be how he made his money. He speculated the man wasn't smart enough to play poker or fly a helicopter.

Well, Mr. Smith, wasn't impressed. He had better things to do with his day than argue with a punk. He looked again at the mirror and twitched his mouth. He would break the mirror before he left with the large dried cow head with feathers hanging in a corner of the room. The cow head seemed out of place in Rio de Janeiro and was something a person would readily find in Arizona. He guessed War Julio bought the object with the painting. Perhaps it was free for purchasing the wretched thing. The man had no taste in art. Maybe the cow head would stick part way into the mirror to reflect the two dead bodies that would soon hit the clay tile floor. There would be very little blood. That was a pity. Poison was sometimes too clean.

The huge ceiling mirror overhead, which fed images from the small video camera to War Julio's computers, were where the police were monitoring. War Julio, Derek, and the police were waiting for the man to speak. He didn't talk which put them on high alert. Something was going down soon. The tension filled the air. The only one relaxed was Mr. Smith who wore a look of consternation and then had a slight smile. He reached for the brass-coated locks and there was a click as each separate lock was released. Mr. Smith stroked the hard and expensive leather of his case like it was his pride and joy.

Inside the briefcase, the police saw the contents as Mr. Smith raised the briefcase lid higher. There were special dart guns containing what looked like five syringes on each gun in a circle with his hellfire killer juice. The police had never seen such a design for a gun. They wondered where it was made. The gun looked professionally molded. The poison was in the cylinders. The gun was designed to single fire or could be fired all at once, and the five syringes would leave a circular pattern of pinpricks. Mr. Smith moved to pick up the special guns. There were two of them, one for each hand.

The police broke into the room. The police shot Mr. Smith in both arms and arrested him. He was taken away to jail. The local attorney could not make bail for him.

It was time to interview the captured criminal and Derek went to the police station. The police searched Smith's Rio apartment and rental vehicle. They found nothing but more syringes with poison and his fake passport. The passport showed his name as John Smith, so they were at a dead end. Derek looked into the deadly green eyes of Jess's monster. She correctly saw his eyes. There were no contacts.

He slowly settled himself in the chair opposite the prisoner. Derek said smoothly, "I'm a Los Angeles investigator here to interview you about your crimes in my country."

The monster tried to stand up and the guards restrained him. He knew all about Derek Wright.

Derek wasn't flustered at all. The reaction of a prisoner being in shackles was always the same. He noted the antagonism emanating from the man. Derek hid his anger as well. The prisoner was now a hostage in a foreign country. The man hadn't counted on that scenario happening.

"I'm only here to ask, why steal the diamond necklace and kill all those people? You know which ones that I'm talking about. I can provide you with their names in case you have forgotten." Nothing came from the prisoner's mouth.

Derek knew this meeting would be a dead end, but he took a long shot. "Also, where's the necklace?"

The prisoner spoke, "Hidden."

Derek stared at the prisoner stonily. Each man measured the other. Derek wouldn't look away. The prisoner looked at the glass and knew others watched through the cloaked screen. He thought of the mirror at the horse estate. He hated clever men. Derek Wright was clever, but the prisoner wasn't going to give him the edge. Smith puffed up his chest like a peacock preening. "Where is your lovely wife? Tell her that I especially enjoyed our private conversation about pink diamonds. She could have gone out to dinner with me any time in Napa. I would have shown her a better time than you did before I killed her. Was she scared when I trashed her room? She wore nice lingerie back then, but you already know about those dainty, see-through items. Elegant and sexy, wouldn't you say?"

Derek stood up with his hands gripped into fists, "Guards, I'm done! Make sure he is always chained."

The prisoner knew that his message rattled the investigator. He intended to do harm. His hatred for the man, personally, was higher now that he was caught. He also hated the wife for other reasons. She halted the Napa robbery by appearing on the scene. The other reason was that he should have been able to connect with her. He decided that she was one of those snobby women.

Mr. Smith wouldn't tell Derek anything other than the one word, *hidden*. The other police received no information from the prisoner.

The prison guards took the poisoner away. Before he left the room, the poisoner yelled, "You're nothing."

Derek left the jail area and drove on the back roads to his pick-up location to take him to the motorboat. He pulled over halfway there and stopped. He pounded on the steering wheel so hard that he thought he would break it. Then he got out of the car and picked up a large stone and threw it in the ocean. "I hope you drown, you miserable, piece of shit. May you hit the streets of hell so hard that your spine cracks." He was a man after all, and sometimes people did get under his skin.

Derek felt better, but knew he would need to calm down a little before talking with his wife. He did, however, tell her the truth because he couldn't help himself. "I wanted to smash Mr. Smith's face in when the stupid criminal asked about you. No, I wanted to kill him right there."

Derek was still angry when he was on the motorboat and explained to Jess everything that transpired in the jail. Jess shook her head because now the necklace seemed to dim in importance. It was time to give up on the mission of retrieving her diamond necklace. The object would be lost forever; she was sure of it. She came over to her husband and snuggled close and put her head on his shoulder. Her eyes misted, and she made herself stop the flow of tears. It was not a good time to cry. She knew that her tears couldn't fix the magic she felt about the necklace. She didn't want Derek to see her pain. She had possibly created, somehow, this disaster. But she was glad dangerous criminals were now halted in their tracks. She could find strength in those circumstances.

Feeling his wife's softness and knowing her actress-mode, he had to give her solutions. There was a way to make things right. It was his responsibility. Willing to buy the other necklace, Derek told her, "We can afford to purchase you the other necklace, if you want. The necklace does matter."

"I love you immensely for your gesture, but that was not necessary because it was not my mother's necklace. A beautiful necklace with Fancy Violet Gray diamonds is in my jewelry box in the safe. I'm a lucky girl to have you. I don't need another necklace. I'm glad the poisoner no longer will exist in our lives after the court trial."

Dean let Derek, one night in a game of poker, win the Fancy Violet Gray necklace she wore for the fake wedding. He felt Jess's reluctance about finding the lost necklace. He did feel relief that the second criminal twin was stopped. There was no way he could escape the shackles. They used the heavy wide ones here. He noticed the link chain had a small space in one of the links. He quickly put the thought out of his mind.

"I love you, too. We can and will continue looking for your mother's necklace when we reach home."

Home was where Jess wanted to be. She needed to see the Hollywood sign on Mount Lee in Los Angeles. It was a silly thought. The sign was only metal, paint, and wood. There were no flashy lights anymore, yet it held a person's attention. The icon suggested richness and aspiration, with a touch of glamour thrown in. She liked the American landmark. She also had enjoyed the famous landmark: Christ the Redeemer. It was a large statue on Corcovado Mountain in Rio and was made of soapstone plus cement. The statue reflected the Christian unity theme and peace. Peace was what she needed and to be back in her own country. Right now, she was tired of chasing her dream. She would love to come back to Rio de Janeiro under better circumstances. Now, it was time to get ready to head home. She would be glad to hear the rumble of the motorboat's engines on its journey. The sound always lulled her into a more relaxed state.

Dean knew War Julio wouldn't be going to Vegas soon for that poker game. He would think about the necklace and the Renaliere woman. It wasn't right that she sold her necklace. Dean had lots of money. There was plenty to purchase a

necklace. He made an important decision. Dean planned his trip
to Italy.

47   Death of Mr. John Smith

THE POLICE PLANNED removal of Mr. John Smith to a small private airstrip where Los Angeles detective, Dave Paulson, would take the handcuffed and chained prisoner to Miami. This would allow Derek two weeks' vacation on the motorboat as it headed back to Los Angeles from Rio. Baby Justin had been flown down by Jim and Mary Beth, who were vacationing in Rio. Jess could be with her husband and child on the return trip. Jim and Mary Beth were going to hook up with some of the Miami husbands and wives.

The two Miami Cortez brothers decided to follow the police van in their rented padded truck to make sure the very seriously evil con artist met the airplane. They didn't want to deal with that poisonous over-five-and-a-half-foot lizard again. They knew all about slippery, scary green-eyed monsters. The rental place where they picked up the truck was called Fish Place from the look of the decrepit sign. They placed their illegally gotten Rio guns with them in the padded truck.

Driving to the airport, the police van suddenly seemed to have a flat tire because it swerved off the road. The police van flipped over, leaving the driver and rider unconscious. The two Miami guys watched Mr. Smith slither out of the van and start walking towards them. The white arm bandages were still in place, but they noticed the jostle of the van caused the wounds to bleed a little. An empty syringe was held in his mouth. They were startled and wondered where the prisoner hid that item. He couldn't possibly have another one they thought.

Worried, the two Miami brothers pulled their guns out because there was no one else on the road. They were fortunate enough to have filled in for the Miami police on occasion as extras. Guns were easily retrievable anywhere. They always chatted with police and prisoners which helped add to their knowledge base about lots of ways to obtain items illegally. Then their Rio friends were also helpful. The two brothers thought *Shoot him first, ask questions later, self-defense.* Then they remembered this was Rio and they didn't know the self-defense rules here and could get in real trouble. They pointed their big plastic guns at the twin con artist, Mr. Smith, and chained him in the back of the rented, padded truck and shut the door. The two Miami guys smelled fish inside the truck before they closed the door.

The two brothers didn't know this area and quickly were lost. They tried to read the map and drive at the same time. The illegal waterproof guns forgotten on the dashboard and the windows were rolled down because the weather was hot. The padded van was going down the hill, and there was a turn up ahead. The padded truck wheel brakes decided to fail, and the boys grabbed their waterproof cell phones and zippered them in their shirts. The truck traveled in space flight over a thirty-foot cliff into the ocean a long distance.

The boys quickly exited the windows, forgetting the waterproof guns that floated away because they were made of some cheap plastic junk. The brothers were high school champion swimmers and swam to shore fast making very little splash waves in the process. The Miami boys knew the creatures that lurked in the ocean.

The padded wooden truck sunk partway in the ocean. The Miami boys reached shore and scrambled up the embankment. They called their wives to pick them up as they somehow walked right back to the airport. They didn't say anything to Dave Paulson, police person at the airport, because they didn't want to cause their families any trouble.

Meanwhile, the padded wooden truck floated partially submerged for a little while and drifted further out into the ocean. It was now directly over this deep trench area of lurking sharks. Dean's huge motorboat was moving a distance away except Dean's crew were always alert to their surroundings. They notified Dean, who brought out his special binocular camera lens, and looked toward the partially submerged wooden truck.

Suddenly, there was a man who crawled out of the top of the truck. The man was in prison garb, still in handcuffs, and with bandages on his arms. He was standing on top of the partially submerged wooden truck. The man was waving his arms frantically. Dean recognized the man as Mr. John Smith. "Fish Place, What the heck?" Derek told Dean about the creep asking about Jess. Dean didn't want the creep on his boat or near Jess. He had to decide. He hoped it was the right one.

Dean refocused and took a close-up photo. He ordered his men to stop the motorboat and lower the small watercraft. He knocked on the third bedroom door, and Derek came out half-dressed. "Watercraft, Smith is in the water." The two men and two of Dean's crew grabbed their guns and climbed into the small watercraft. They steered toward the partially submerged wooden truck. The large motorboat was turning around to drop anchor.

The motorboat was a distance out, keeping to deep water. The wooden truck sunk a little further into the ocean now half-submerged. The small watercraft was approximately six hundred yards away. Suddenly, the truck slowly tipped, throwing the waving man who now became a thrashing man into the ocean.

The thrashing and yelling alerted the school of sharks plus the smell of fish. The sharks were mad when they saw the truck descending upon them in their favorite spot in their own territory. The sharks dodged around the truck, and then they saw the lizard in the water. There was something wrong with the lizard, so the sharks moved closer. Next the sharks smelled the arms. The sharks knew this smell: blood. They opened their mouths to show rows of very sharp teeth and raced each other to the main attraction for today. In less than a minute, there was no more Mr. Smith.

The small watercraft circled and saw a ring of red-colored water and the truck sinking deeper. The sharks moved away to find another place. One of Dean's crew members was holding a shark repellent gun. The outside paper wrapper read, "Shark Repellent 500 Yards." The inner canister was gone. The crew member said, "Sorry, boss, we used the canister at the last gunfire show with that bozo in the water. We forgot to put a new one in." Dean was relieved.

They returned the small watercraft to the anchored motorboat. Dean showed Derek the photo of the person on top of the truck. Derek said, "It's the deadly green-eyed prisoner. It's the monster, who is nothing now to anyone. He lost his sick life." Dean nodded and patted Derek on the shoulders. They agreed not to show Jess the photo. It was nightmare enough looking at the creepy photo.

Derek called Paulson at the small airport who thought Mr. Smith escaped from the police van. The police van was found with the unconscious people who were taken to the hospital. There was no sign of Mr. Smith. Derek loaded the camera photo into the computer and sent the photo of Mr. Smith's last few minutes. He was pleased there would be no trial with the obsessed reptile, and Jess was safely sheltered from his poisonous and crude male mind. He explained to Paulson what happened. He gave Paulson the location of the now totally submerged Fish Place van.

The chef on the motorboat made shark for dinner. Tonight, was chef's choice night. Dean liked to give the chef freedom in the motorboat kitchen once a week. He had forgotten which night it was. The shark looked and smelled delicious. Dean asked the chef, "Was the shark from Rio?"

"No, sir, absolutely not. The chefs know their shark is not that tasty. This shark is from a fishing company in Curacao. Their fish is the best, always fresh, expertly cut, and clean."

Derek started laughing. Jess joined in. Dean thought, *Finally*.

Dean and the crew could now relax. Dean started laughing. The scale tipped back to normal partially due to his crew. There was justice in this world after all.

Dean told his chef, "Bring two bottles of our best champagne with the chocolate mousse dessert. It's time for a celebration. I plan on giving my crew a bonus after the trip. The amount just went up higher."

Later they learned the padded Fish Place van was stolen. It was parked next to the Fiske Place rental padded van. The fish man left his keys in his fish truck. The rental shop received cash from some customers to rent their padded van, but the customers never took it off the lot. The rental shop sign read Fiske Place, but one of the weathered boards on the sign had fallen off.

There were no cameras in the rental shop and the sales clerk couldn't remember a thing about them. She was American and thought they were, absolutely, two guys from Rio. She thought one of them spoke Portuguese or Spanish. She didn't know either language, but they didn't speak English at all. The two guys' just hand-motioned to her and pointed to their rental truck. They gave her extra cash. The signature on the rental form read, "GLO0000".

Dean figured it was the Cortez brothers from Miami. They heard about the San Francisco arrest story from Tami, one of the guy's wife, and thought the license plate incident was funny. Dean knew they meant no harm, somehow picked up the con artist, missed the airport road, and the brakes failed because it was the wrong padded truck.

The two boys could be considered semi-heroes. They were in the right place at the right time; the con artist was not. Wrong turn, wrong brakes, wrong padded truck, and wrong shark repellent canister turned the situation around. The sharks were the heroes that ended the terror. They ripped the evil lizard into fish food.

Dean's coffee accidentally spilled on the signature line of the rental agreement before the police read it. The red tape to correct the issue would take too long in a foreign country, not to mention the cost. He knew a judge would eventually exonerate them. Therefore, he saved everybody time and money. He also owed Tami a marker favor for the photo of the diamond necklace in Rio. He paid his markers in full.

Dean also felt a little guilty. The captain hadn't heard him say his *now* command. Consequently, the captain didn't use the thrusters full force to slow down the motorboat quicker. When he and Derek walked through the equipment room to board the watercraft, he saw the shark repellent canisters. He could have grabbed an extra one, which he usually did. This time he didn't. Instead, he watched Derek put on his windbreaker before entering the small boat. The watercraft engine appeared to slow before reaching the flailing prisoner. There was enough of a delay.

Did he tip the scale? He felt that he put his finger on it some. Jess would now be free from the two men who stalked her. This was a good thing. He didn't regret any of his actions or was it inactions? Dean knew that sometimes a person's conscience put a blindfold on during stress. This time, maybe fate stepped in. He thought about the Statue of Liberty. Her torch lighted the way to freedom. He thought fate, which carried its own light. Perhaps fate was just waiting to get a chance at Mr. Smith and took advantage of a perfect moment. Dean felt tired. Maybe his logic was a little constrained by recent events.

Then, he said to himself, no. The two creatures didn't deserve freedom in a great American jail. It was the bad guy's time to go. Hell, or some other non-earth entity was waiting for the reptile and the other twin. It was their time to end on this earth.

48   Officer Simms and Vineyards

OFFICER SIMMS CONTACTED Jess on her cell phone. The little boy Justin was now three years old, and she was five months pregnant with a little girl, whom she and Derek agreed to call, Sami, after her real mother. Officer Simms was disappointed because she had not been back to Napa to drink their terrible office coffee. He told her that he was glad they caught poison boy. Simms asked her, "How did you know where to find him?"

"We didn't; it was just something we accidentally stepped on."

Simms squinted his eyes and said, "Yeah, right, only this time I believe you."

Then Simms asked for Derek, and they had a nice conversation. Jess heard them talk about fishing before she went down below deck as Justin had awakened from his nap

Simms told Derek that he sure enjoyed the fishing boat trip with Jim. They both caught their limit of Stripers, and a couple of them were seven pounders. He mentioned that Jim was one heck of a fun guy.

"You should see all his fishing lures. There must have been over a hundred, at least. I made him leave the smaller ones in his trunk and guess what? His trunk still contains the storage of his rifle with impressive scope, plus all the odd gear. I thought he built a garage to store the stuff. Well, maybe not. You remember his rifle. I wish I owned one. To get back to the fishing, there is no use stringing small lures on an ocean pole. Huge fish in the ocean will swallow it and spit the thing out like a disastrous minnow. Jim showed me this faded lure that I thought was no good. He should have left it at the store he bought it from. I wouldn't have purchased it. Not me. I couldn't believe that he caught this huge Striper fish on a faded green lure with orange stripes. It was the big fish of the day. He told me that it was his favorite. He bought the lure on a trip for a special client. He wouldn't tell me the client's name and clammed up. The fish catch was good. We've agreed to return next year for another go at it, but enough of my jawing. Let's get to the important reason that I called you."

Derek told him that he was glad they didn't get skunked. Jim, obviously, was better at fishing than he was at poker.

That made Simms chortle with delight. "I'll have to rib him about the poker. Hey, I can probably win that faded lure. Thanks a million."

"Anytime," said Derek. "Oh, and good luck getting that faded lure from Jim. I know his special client." He was enjoying the call already. Let Jim tell him the story about the lure. He had liked Simms from the start of the Napa investigation.

Simms explained to Derek, "A grape picker found this aluminum box at the end of a grape vineyard field. The Napa area was delivered with some heavy rain that washed away the sand to reveal the edge of the box. The worker gave the box to the owner, who was a good friend. The owner knew about the Napa Jewelry store robbery, murders of Mr. and Mrs. Beacon, and the store's illegal bait-and-switch tactics on out-of-town visitors. The owner didn't like crime to ruin his ability to sell his wine. He called the criminals rabbit-turds. You see, he had problems with furry scavengers in his vineyards and would let the dogs scare the dickens out of them. Jim's rifle sure could have solved the over-rabbit population in a hurry. Oh, there's also lots of hippies here that believe in the Chinese zodiac stuff. You know, the year of the Rabbit was 2016. I read somewhere that rabbits are serene and calm. Sure, they are happy when they have all those grape leaves stuffed in their mouth. The rabbits are high on fructose and the chlorophyll is a carb-heaven. My friend couldn't believe it when his friends in Helena put a huge metal sculpture of the darn rabbit on their vineyard grounds. He figured the vineyard owner gave up and put in a whole field of grapes just for the critters. Meanwhile, my friend is still fighting them rabbits. He wasn't about to give up an inch of his fields. He did, however, think it was a good move to sell wine. The metal rabbit was a gimmick that worked for his friends. He wished them luck. My friend's word is an apt description for the criminals. I was thinking lots of other cuss words. Morons was on the safe side compared to what names stuck."

Derek waited patiently for Simms and then gave up.

"Simms, what about the box?" asked Derek.

"Oh, yeah. The box is important! It was as good as finding Jim with his schoolteacher in the cave. That darn door sealed them in just like a box and we had no idea how to open the heavy door. Jim slid me the key. He made my day."

Derek coughed into the phone.

"Right, let me move onward. The owner asked if we could mention his winery's name in the newspaper article regarding the diamond necklace and how he would be forever grateful. I assured my good friend that we can."

Derek sat up straighter at full attention.

"You said diamond necklace? Was there a necklace in the aluminum box? Is it Jess's?"

"Absolutely, that's what I've been trying to tell you. My friend, the Napa vineyard owner, delightedly brought the diamonds to the police station. Inside the box was a leather pouch that contained a diamond necklace with a strange clasp. It matched the picture the police had of the artist's sketch on one of the stolen items. Now, if Jess could identify that necklace and complete some paperwork, she could come pick the item up in Napa. The police were tired of moving that box around and wanted to return the beautiful item to the correct owner. We haven't found any of the other stolen items and believe they disappeared in the belly of the underworld."

Simms sent Derek the picture of the necklace, and he included a shot of himself and Jim holding a string of Stripers.

Simms mentioned as a sideline that Rutherford was no longer with them. She left to work as a prison counselor. She needed to be closer to her sister.

Derek said, "Thanks for keeping me up-to-date. The necklace is a huge, impressive find. I must keep this trip to Napa as a surprise for Jess."

Simms was all right with the surprise. Derek explained his plan, and set the date for next week. He let Jim and Dean know about the deliverance of the diamond necklace.

Jess was delighted that she and Derek were staying the weekend in Napa. She was glad he was taking a break. He sent her off to buy some pretty evening clothes. First, they must stop at the police department to talk with Simms.

Then they would head to Yountville for dinner at their favorite restaurant. Jess put her backpack of camera, lenses, night vision binoculars and the rest of her gear just like Derek knew she would. She kept her jeweler's tools in her handbag.

Simms welcomed them back to Napa and took them into his office. He had the forms ready. He took out the leather pouch from a locked drawer and handed it to Jess. Jess removed the diamond necklace from the pouch and looked at the clasp.

She told Simms, "The necklace contains an inside to the clasp. Her mother's name is Samantha and I called her Sami when I was little. She passed away a long time ago. My father recently died and told me the story about our family heirloom, which I believe, is this very necklace. My mother saved the Renaliere's child from drowning while my father and she visited Italy. The inside inscription should read, 'To Sami from the Renaliere's.'"

Jess opened her jeweler's tools. She touched the clasp in the exact spot the old woman showed her. She took her magnifier and gave the necklace and object to Simms. Simms read the inscription and handed back the diamond necklace.

Simms said, "Here's your stolen necklace, Jess. The adopted son showed us an old picture that he found stuffed into a shoebox. His mother kept the picture hidden from him and other people all these years. The woman in the picture was wearing a diamond necklace. It is a picture of your mother. We compared this black and white photo to her driver's license photo. The facial recognition match shows the two people are one and the same."

Simms handed Jess the black and white photograph. The picture was of her mother. She nodded.

"It's now your family's heirloom again. Congratulations."

Jess signed the forms. She hugged Simms and told him goodbye.

Then she and Derek drove to Yountville. Derek opened her car door, and Jess fell in his arms, crying. Derek held her a long time. It was part of the healing that needed to happen for Jess. It was important. Dean informed him of that important fact. Derek told him he figured that solution out sitting in the condo in San Francisco without her.

Finally, they ate dinner in the restaurant and ordered oysters from Tomales Bay for appetizers. The chef prepared them in a special warm butter garlic sauce. Jess ate her Caesar salad and steak and lifted some forks for later to use on Derek. She would return them, of course, with an apology.

Their weekend was sweet memories and extra special. The two of them attended the opera in San Francisco Saturday evening, and Jess wore her newly found necklace and gorgeous navy satin designer gown. Some of the cronies were there at the opera with their wives. Dean called in extra protection just in case. He was taking no chances. He wanted them to have a great time.

Jess and Derek went to the small chapel for Sunday service before flying back to Los Angeles.

49   Birth of Sami

IT WAS TIME to deliver their baby, and they hurried to the hospital. Derek and Jess bought a beautiful home with a view of the ocean, country club, and the rest of the good life in California. Derek drove her toward the hospital, and they handed over a sleepy Justin to Jim and Mary Beth. Dean was on his way to the hospital. Derek suddenly had a flat tire, and Dean picked the two of them up to take Jess to the hospital. The flat tire freaked Derek some. He was nervous and jumpy. This was still a foreign experience for him. Dean told him that he needed to relax.

They arrived at the emergency room and the intern approached. His name tag said, "John Smith."

It was the same name as the creepy poisoner. Derek wheeled her out of that hospital so fast Dean had to run. Derek told Dean, "Call her doctor to meet us at the boat dock by the motorboat."

Derek told Jess, "You need to hold it inside."

Jess tried real hard, but she delivered Sami in the third bedroom before the doctor arrived. The doctor checked mother and the baby out. They were both fine. He would return in the morning. Jess was tired and happy, holding her fuzzy blonde, beautiful baby girl. Dean came in and asked if he could show her around his luxurious motorboat, aka the tub. Jess let him.

She and Derek were alone. "Don't ever have a baby that fast again. I thought my heart stopped."

"Don't freak out when you see that dead con artist's name. A person couldn't hold a baby inside when it's ready. Having a baby is like a train charging a station. All the lights

199

said stop, but the train said no way. Train wins every time. You went berserk when you saw that name and became irrational. You need to calm down. The baby and I are safe. Are you clear on that subject?"

Jess was right. Derek knew she was right.

Baby Sami was a doll. It took all of Jess and Derek's efforts to provide her and Justin a near normal childhood. But then nothing was ever normal in their household. There was the huge baby shower for Sami at two in the afternoon on Dean's boat that turned into a wedding party for Jim and Mary Beth at seven in the evening. All the cronies from San Francisco and Miami with wives were invited, along with three city police departments.

The baby shower brought a jungle of animals, baby clothes, and paraphernalia, which they put in one of the super nets to make room for the guests. There were so many balloons that the crew who had tied them to the helicopter were worried every time the wind picked up. The combination balloon package formed this huge sail.

There were competition games off the back end of the boat with the shark repellent guns. The sharks moved permanently to the Farallon Islands by San Francisco close to the two nuclear waste dumpsites. The two parties in this area were too much for the sharks.

Jess wore a new designer white gown from Paris that the ladies liked. She gave them the designer's name who was flooded with orders. Jess was invited back by the designer for next year's show, all expenses already paid in advance.

Dean and the cronies were trying to figure out the favor-marker scale as to who owed whom what. By the end of the party, Dean didn't owe anyone any markers due to his expert poker hand. Dean even invited War Julio, who learned how to bluff in a poker game. War Julio also learned the marker business.

The War Julio people were examining all the mirrors on Dean's boat until they met the Miami fence's daughters. It was one totally amazing day. Some of the Miami fence's daughters moved to Rio and Curacao, so the underworld connection grew stronger, more global. The fish business grew even bigger for War Julio. He married one of the Miami daughters and helped expand his world.

50   Problem with Dean

SEVERAL YEARS PASSED. Dean kept having pains in his chest and finally went to see his doctor. He had major health issues. The doctor gave him medicine and sent him home, which now was permanently on his beloved motorboat. He sold his condo about the time Jess and Derek bought their home.

He started looking back upon his life and knew his life had been dull. The occasional poker game was a temporary high. His life changed the day he met Jess. Then she introduced him to Derek and Jim. He laughed because it had been a magical ride. Dean called his lawyer to visit him on the boat, and they crafted his will. There was plenty of money to go around. He had done well.

Dean passed away, and there was no funeral. His body became an urn of ashes that Derek, Jess, and Jim took out twelve miles from shore and threw into the ocean, along with a stack of poker chips. The will gave Jim enough money to purchase a fishing tub with dock fees paid for ten years at a local yacht club.

The cronies were each given one hundred thousand dollars with a note that they spend it in Vegas with their wives.

Dean purchased the necklace from War Julio for the price he paid for it and gave the family Renaliere the necklace back.

He gave his accountant and lawyer some money. He left money to various schools and universities. He donated money to various police charities. There was also money left to a few madam prostitutes. Two gray ducks mysteriously arrived at the chicken farmer's yard one day. There must have been a private note from Dean to someone in his crony families about the repayment of those ducks.

He left the motorboat to Jess and Derek with paid maintenance and dock fees for ten years with a stipulation. The stipulation was that they have a party on the motorboat with his friends and fireworks on the anniversary of his death. He left a fund specifically for this task and his funeral party. The other stipulation was that they keep his crew onboard for as long as they wanted, and he set up a fund for that.

The funeral party on the motorboat was huge. Everyone left except the crew. The fireworks display was done except for a special fireworks package for Jess and Derek after the party was over. Included was a very old bottle of scotch. Jess and Derek poured their glass of scotch and told the firework's guy they were ready.

There was a beautiful colorful display and then the last display, which looked like the diamond necklace. Derek held Jess in his arms.

"I love your body touching my warm body. I'm enormously glad everyone is safe, especially you. We found something very rare, special, and it isn't the necklace or money. It isn't about who is stronger. It's how we could combine our strength into a stronger relationship, a stronger bond called love."

"That was what Dean was trying to help us find. He knew about love, because he had been there. He wanted us to arrive at that magical place. I'm glad we made it."

51   Sami's Drawing and Vision

IT HAD BEEN over a year since Dean passed away. Jess was playing with Justin and Sami in the lower lounge of the boat. A specially designed motorboat that Dean ordered and left for Justin was a favorite toy. It was a mini replica of the large motorboat. Sami helped him play chase with the little Jet Skis. Derek told Justin a soft version of some of the stories with Dean. Justin wanted to grow up and be like Derek and Dean. Also like Jim. The boy knew solid role models.

Then Sami got out her papers for coloring. She drew a picture of the diamond necklace because her mother told her the story and let her hold the beautiful object. Sami knew all about diamonds and knew all her mother's jewelry. She had good role models, too. She was around very strong, capable women helping her every step of the way. Both children would do well out in the crazy world.

Suddenly, Jess threw one of the fish pillows at Justin. Justin picked up the octopus pillow and threw it at Sami. Then all three of them were screaming, laughing, throwing pillows, and running around the lower lounge. The three were putting up lots of noise.

Two crew members realized they were just playing. The young crew member said, "Boy, they were super noisy." The older crew man laughed. "No, this noise was nothing like the night they caught some of the bad guys."

So, the older crew man told him the story that was beyond, beyond super noisy. The noise could be heard for fifty miles surrounding the motorboat. All the gunfire and lights were some laser show kicked up a notch.

Then there were two crazy other locations, one with more gunfire and the other one a dune buggy and heavy barbed wire. The barbed wire was the same heavy gage that was used to seal up the caves in the area by the police. One of those bails of wire was stolen. It was found strung all over this private beach road. No one knew how the wire arrived there. They found several straw scarecrows, too. That surprised the police as there were no crops in the area. They figured teenagers were having a Halloween or beer party with those straw dummies.

The two children and adults quieted down. Sami brought the paper picture necklace to Jess. Jess told her sweet daughter, "The picture is a beautiful one."

Her child drew the necklace with the clasp including the ridge, but this time she had drawn the setting not in the gray crayon, but in the gold crayon. All the child's prior drawings were in gray. Jess asked her daughter, "Why did you color the setting in gold and there was some green on the clasp?"

"I saw it in my head and liked the diamond necklace that way. It's the origin."

Jess said, "You mean the original?"

Her daughter shook her head, "Yes".

Jess thought that this was a new experience. She asked her daughter if anyone had shown her a picture or the necklace in the gold setting.

"No. It was just up there in my head. I saw it in my head, but the necklace was stuck."

She pondered about telling Derek. Jess knew he would go berserk, and then she would have to calm him down. She said to herself, let me rethink this one, calming my husband down might be fun. Jess would table this new development a tiny bit. She needed a little time. She told herself that it was the female way of making things better. She could almost hear Dean cough and shake his head. He was still with her, correcting her thoughts.

52   Auction Brochure

DEREK RECEIVED AN envelope from Dean's lawyer.
Derek was told he must only open the envelope with Jess
present. Derek figured it was some private note arranged by
Dean. He finished his workday and went home to their ocean
view home. Jess said, "How was your day honey?"

The message was a familiar one between them. Derek
grinned and showed her the envelope in his hand. She saw the
attorney's name and felt some anxiety about the envelope.
Thinking about Dean the other day when the children were
playing and now this. What could be in the envelope? Jess told
him they would open it later after their children were in bed.
Both Derek and Jess were quiet at the dinner table, wondering
about the envelope. The children didn't mind and were busy
chattering their stories to their parents, giving them a wonderful
glimpse into their free, safe, young world.

Derek opened the envelope and started reading Dean's
letter.

> Dear Jess and Derek,
>
> Kiss the little ones for me as I surely miss
> them. I hope the funeral party was a heck of a good
> time. I miss those times too. I miss Derek but not that
> much. I miss Jess very, very much. I hope you enjoy
> the motorboat. The brochure was something given to
> me by War Julio. There was a small oil painting of a
> young woman. The painting belonged to the Renaliere
> family. The young woman was their great-great-
> grandmother. The family auctioned off the painting in
> Rome due to their almost bankrupt state.
>
> War Julio was going to purchase the painting
> but chose another one instead. The brochure

contained a picture of the painting. I thought you would be interested in seeing the painting. I did some research with the Auction House. There was a story about this painting. It included that *something* word that Jess seemed to run into most of the time. The story included a robbery, and the robber escaped on a ship, which hit terrible seas in the Atlantic Ocean, and the ship went down. The entire crew and all the goods onboard were never found.

The location that the officials thought the ship went down was somewhere around the West coast of Africa near Freetown in Sierra Leone. That was what the Renaliere family was told. If you remember from your school education, in the 1700s there were ships that went there for the slave trade. There also is 250 miles of coastline around Sierra Leone.

The Auction House included the name and address of the buyer of the painting--with his permission, of course. It was an elderly gentleman who bought the painting for his wife who saw it at the auction. I wish you luck on your next journey. I will be with you every step of the way, relaxing. Guess what the robber stole? I thought it was something.
Love, Dean

Jess opened the brochure and flipped through the painting section. She found the oil painting of the young woman. Jess saw what the stolen item was and couldn't believe it. Derek looked at the painting and saw only the woman.

Jess brought out her magnifier and grabbed the brochure. The woman was wearing a diamond necklace. The clasp was pinned to the side with a diamond bar holding the clasp into the angled slots on the bar pin.

The diamond necklace and clasp were almost an exact replica of Jess's diamond necklace. The necklace was not set in platinum, but was set in gold. Jess sat back in awe. She handed Derek the magnifier. Derek saw the necklace and said, "Sami's gold necklace drawing. Unbelievable coincidence."

They both started laughing as Dean gave them a gift. He knew they would take their vacations in the future and check out the painting and possibly the African coastline. Derek and Jess also knew the dangers. They would need to redo their wills just in case to protect their children.

Inside of the envelope was a key to one of Dean's many owned and leased collections of warehouses. The revenue stream from the massive holdings was over $1,750,000 per year after expenses. The warehouse holdings were just a small part of the network of holdings that Dean accumulated and left to Jess and Derek.

Derek could have retired, but he told Jess, "I like to catch the bad guy, the con artist." Jess remembered Napa when he mentioned to her those exact words. She couldn't change the person that he was inside, and he couldn't change her. The two of them reached a truce a long time ago. Derek would stand by Jess. Jess would stand by him. They finally went to the warehouse number.

Inside was a two-man sub, fully equipped, all kinds of diving gear and business cards to classes, instructors, and sub installers for the motorboat. The warehouse contained new guidance system maps of the African coast and names of contacts and phone numbers for them along the coast.

Dean obviously researched and checked out the company backgrounds ahead, exploring all the possibilities for them. He even left the Miami contacts, and included on the list was War Julio.

Jess turned to Derek, "Is he in?"

Derek saw her determined look. "He's in."

Derek would follow her through the gates of hell and out the other side to protect her. He was going full throttle into their next possible plan. He learned from Dean. Jess entered the game and became the main attraction. All the thugs would think they were safe and lead Jess to the fiery gates. Jess would walk them inside and find an exit plan.

Derek was a smart guy. He wanted to be on Jess's team. It was the same with Dean. He figured everything out the day he met Jess.

53 Visiting Louisa Renaliere

THE NEXT MONTH, Derek and Jess headed to Rome, Italy, with their children and nanny in tow for two weeks' vacation. They planned to visit the old gentleman who bought the painting so that they could view it up close. The children were brought along because the vacation was truly for relaxation and fun.

It was to be a fact-finding mission as they also planned to meet with the last remaining Renaliere family member. The little girl Sami wanted to know when she could meet Mrs. Louisa Renaliere. Jess and Derek hadn't told Sami the lady's first name, nor had they discussed the name anywhere in her presence or their boat crew or anyone close to them. Derek was astounded.

Louisa was in a small three-bedroom apartment with antique furniture, paintings, old crystal, and beautiful Persian rugs. They were surprised to see she kept a butler. The door to the kitchen was partially open, and their daughter, Sami, saw the butler's son before he closed the door. When they met Louisa, the little girl and the elderly lady became best friends. Louisa was old but was smart and efficient.

Louisa bought the paste version of her diamond necklace online at a computer website that sold inexpensive old jewelry. The San Francisco police had given the paste necklace back to the adopted son, who quickly sold it to an antique store because he didn't want to be reminded of the murder or the fact that his mother stole it. He wanted nothing to do with that horrible necklace.

The website contained links to lots of antique stores around the world. Louisa heard about such an item and went looking for the fake necklace every day until she found it. She already switched the necklaces, putting the paste one in her wall safe. Her real diamond necklace was in the vault at her bank. She gave the key to her bank box to her lawyer with a new will.

Sami whispered, "You shouldn't trust the man in the kitchen."

Louisa told Sami, "You should not worry because things are already covered."

Sami smiled.

Louisa told Jess and Derek, "Sami is a good spirit."

Derek thought the woman was talking about Jess's mother, Samantha. Jess knew she was talking about their daughter.

Jess said that one word: *magical.*

The old woman nodded. Derek saw the nod and knew the word. He would talk to Jess about this conversation later this evening after they had made love. Even Justin was hugged and loved by the woman. The old woman fused over both of their children. The old woman told them she loved family. She even mentioned family many more times.

Jess and Derek received enough information from Louisa to plan their next year's vacation. This information was hidden within the family for at least a century or so. Jess felt the strength from the old woman and her daughter. The bond was there and powered energy strong between the three females.

She could not tell anyone. She promised the old woman, and she was glad to leave the old woman's apartment.

Derek and Jess saw the wonderful oil painting of the exquisite gold diamond necklace and *stuck* pin. The necklace was the original one which belonged to the great-great-grandmother of the Renaliere family in the 1700s. The necklace was also the stolen one, still lost to the family. The robber escaped with their special old chest where the jewels were stored. To Louisa, it wasn't the current price but memories of family.

The diamonds in the necklace were all larger stones. The clasp was larger and contained bigger stones on the face than Jess's necklace. The stones in the clasp were emeralds. Along with the necklace that was stolen was a gold and diamond diadem or hair ornament.

Louisa told them what was inside the clasp of the necklace before the man in the kitchen listened to the rest of their conversation. "Inside the clasp are more emeralds."

The gold diamond and emerald necklace, diamond pin, and diamond diadem were in a separate compartment at the bottom of the box.

The old woman leaned over to Jess, "I must explain to you the lock mechanism and how to access the necklace hidden section of the box. The locked oak box is lined with two layers of brass along with twenty coins that the family acquired. The coins are rare. The coins were from Syracuse on the island of Sicily designed by the engraver Kimon. He was the finest of the ancient engravers and chose Arethusa on one of the sides of the coin. He chose her because she was beautiful and stunning, of course. Kimon worked hard to catch the essence of woman.

"The coin from five hundred fifteen BC was a tetradrachm with the facing head of Arethusa. This Arethusa is a fictitious creature of water. The coin is signed on both the obverse and reverse. Some dealers say the coin is valued at current day price of one hundred eighty thousand dollars each. Because the coins were a collection, the price would probably be higher for the twenty coins. The ship was registered in 1725 as a slave ship, but the investigator at the great-great-grandmother's time, thought it was more a smuggling stolen goods trade vessel. What was on the sunken ship could be only the objects stolen that belonged to our family or more."

Louisa looked tired from unloading her burden of family secrets. Jess heated her tea in an old mug and put it back into the dainty cup for her. Jess brought back the tea.

Next Louisa said, "The investigator thought the ship contained more. More something. Very much more valuable and precious something. The Italians wanted to find that very specific ship a long time ago and were searching around Freetown, the now Republic of Sierra Lione. The cargo was important said the investigator. The investigator was a good friend whose family had known the Renaliere family for generations."

"The investigator found additional information about the ship and was told it just left Goree Island after picking up strong slaves which were needed to eventually unload the cargo. Some sailing trawler-type vessel in the area thought they saw a ship go down. The fisherman who saw the ship, was about four days' ride out of Dakar. They didn't check it out because a storm approached rapidly. They already pulled up their trawl nets. Their boat was full of fish and they moved to safety."

Derek said, "But Goree Island was off the coast of Dakar, the now Republic of Senegal."

"Yes, that's exactly right," said Louisa.

Louisa told them, "The Italians possibly were searching the wrong area. The investigator friend gave her family a single draw mahogany ship's scope with a segmented draw tube for access to the lenses. Their investigator friend was murdered on his way back to the officials. That was why her great-great-grandmother wasn't sure that piece of information reached the Italians."

Louisa retrieved a small key off this old gold intricate chain she wore and went to her bookcase. Her aurum necklace was her favorite and she wore it always. She brought out the scope and gave it to Derek as a gift.

She leaned over and told them, "There's a small paper inside the lenses."

Louisa leaned over again and whispered some more information.

Jess and Derek looked at each other, "The cargo was that something word."

When they were back at their hotel, Derek undid the segmented draw. Inside was a piece of old papyrus with barely distinguishable writing. Derek recognized the three different sets of figures, which were coordinates written on the paper. He pulled up the three different coordinates on his computer and sent himself a note with the coordinate information. Then he placed the small old paper back inside the scope.

54 Butler's Son

WHENEVER THE WORD *diamonds* are mentioned, you can bet on there being someone listening. Diamonds or the word, woman, brought visions of stars. The two objects raised the psyche of men. Either one of those objects were part of the forbidden world ever since Eve ate the apple or men found the precious gem. Evolution couldn't erase their powerful pull.

The argument would always start as to which one was more important. Each person had their own opinion. There was the love-hate relationship on both. The importance of value depended upon which tyrannical world held the criminal's fancy.

No one cared about the mess involved in grabbing onto either of the stars, except the diamonds were usually more tangible. Whereas a woman, she could be as unreachable as all get-out. The criminal took the lesser challenge. The want of diamonds never stopped. Revolutions were skirted, because the criminal cause was more important. Revolutions could wait. The bad guy wasn't into politics or religion.

Even in jail, the criminals would tell you that they would steal and do everything all over again. The mention of a potential treasure evoked images of intrigue. They saw riches. Riches were their air.

Which one of the groups, departments, or levels of con artist was listening comes to mind? How extreme was their obsession? Only they knew. Cyclone force may be the wind speed of their obsession and others.

The woman's butler had a son, who was visiting his father. His name was Stew Avery. He caught part of Jess,

Derek, and Louisa's conversation. He also saw the exchange of the brass ship's scope. He pondered about that antique. He had never paid it any mind. Could it be more valuable than he knew? His assessment was only one hundred dollars. What if he was wrong? Questions rattled his brain.

The butler's son was a small con artist. In the past, it was small items that he could steal without anyone knowing. The old woman would have known had he tried to steal the telescope. However, he obtained enough information from listening secretly to begin his search for the worth-a-fortune, original diamond and gold necklace.

Stew's very con artist eyes glittered much like the sunken diamond and emerald necklace had in its height of gentility and knights. This con artist was on the opposite spectrum from true knights. He was no warrior and would have to hire newbie con thieves for help. The newbies knew a very smart and wealthy con artist in Africa.

Stew was doing absolutely nothing for the moment. There was enough time and he could always steal Louisa's diamond necklace with the platinum setting from her wall safe for additional money. He didn't like Louisa anyway, and the feelings were mutual on her end. The evil con artist person jumped to take the advantage, armed with this new knowledge.

The man contacted the fence he knew in Africa. He needed someone with money to fund the expedition. He could feel the pull of money and all it could buy. He was walking taller already. Stew crossed over to the other side of the game.

The butler's son saw his father's unhappy face. He kept wiping his brow from nervousness, and he turned the heat higher in Louisa's condo. The butler, obviously, didn't want her to die or he would be out of a job.

Stew wore his normal strange expression and ignored his father. His father once told him that he was trouble. Stew thought it a joke that his father wanted to name him, Declan. He looked it up and found the meaning of the name meant *nothing*. That was when Stew decided to become rich.

Louisa was old, but not stupid. She saw the evil complicated look in the butler's son, and she made plans of her own. No shadowed devil ghost was going to catch her napping. The Wrights were a great team, and she would always be on their side. It was the side of good. Her spirit was prepared for the fight. She kept a bland, serene face so that the butler's son wouldn't catch onto her thoughts. She could play the game of deception, too.

The devil's teeth or some other foreign entity's teeth were grinding, plans were being laid, and the flames were building. No coal was required. Stew had entered the game.

"Who would win?" It was hard to tell as the scales were currently out of balance due to the windy climate which caused air to be under duress in earth's atmosphere. No one was sorry the scales couldn't balance. That meant an open door to greed. Mess was going to happen. The stars were waiting, brilliant, sparkly, and far away.

"*Come get me,*" called the diamonds.

Others would enter the game, willingly. They saw signs and heard things through the underground. Riches would even the game, they were sure. More deceit and outrageous happenings would be on the horizon. But, they didn't know the coordinates.

"Or did they?"

The old ship's scope held *something.*

No one really knew but they would take a gamble. The fiends would talk to their friends who were more criminals. Criminals knew all about coordinates. Things would start happening. The ocean would fill with another diving ship from Africa.

217